a life, forward

also by Tracy Hewitt Meyer

A Life, Redefined
The Reformation of Marli Meade

a Rowan Slone novel

TRACY HEWITT MEYER

Livonia, Michigan

Editor: Joni Firestone
Proofreader: Rebecca Rue

A LIFE, FORWARD
Copyright © 2020 Tracy Hewitt Meyer
All rights reserved. No part of this publication may be reproduced, distributed, or transmitted in any form or by any means, including photocopying, recording, or other electronic or mechanical methods, without the prior written permission of the publisher, except in the case of brief quotations embodied in critical reviews and certain other noncommercial uses permitted by copyright law. For permission requests, please write to the publisher.

This book is a work of fiction. The characters, incidents, and dialogue are drawn from the author's imagination and are not to be construed as real. Any resemblance to actual events or persons, living or dead, is entirely coincidental.

Published by BHC Press

Library of Congress Control Number: 2017941232

ISBN: 978-1-64397-150-6 (Hardcover)
ISBN: 978-1-64397-152-0 (Softcover)
ISBN: 978-1-64397-153-7 (Ebook)

For information, write:
BHC Press
885 Penniman #5505
Plymouth, MI 48170

Visit the publisher:
www.bhcpress.com

*for Kate Marie,
may you always find strength, love
and peace within yourself*

Light.
It shines ahead.
A glimmer. A flash.
Then it is gone.
Like it never existed.
But I saw it.
And it changed me.
~ Rowan Slone ~

 a life, forward

chapter one

MY BREATH formed tiny crystals as I left the animal shelter after another day at work. Janie, my boss, was still inside closing up for the day. I wanted to ask to leave early so I could see my boyfriend, Mike, who was supposed to be coming home from college. The only problem was he had been promising this since August. It was now January. I had only seen him once, and I didn't want to get my hopes up.

He should have been home right before Christmas, the same night he finished his last final. But a player on his soccer team got hurt, and Mike took his place at an indoor tournament. He should've been home Thanksgiving, but his soccer team entered a last minute scrimmage against another school. The same story had repeated itself too many times to count.

I was happy for Mike.

I was heartbroken for me.

My teeth chattered, and my hand shook as I tried to unlock the car door. It was dark out, clouds obscuring the stars, the moon. The trees that peppered the rural landscape were bare and stark.

I whispered a prayer that the snow would hold off until he got home, assuming he had actually left the university town five hours away. A string of possible excuses marched through my head, but I immediately dismissed them. He would come home this time.

The streets were empty except for two pickup trucks hauling muddy four-wheelers. Despite my best effort not to get excited and end up disappointed again, I pushed my foot on the gas and sped toward the only home I had known since last May.

The Andersons lived in a typical upper middle-class neighborhood where the lawns were green, the weeds didn't grow, and the streetlights never seemed to burn out. Row after row of two-story, redbrick homes sat stoically along the tree-lined streets. The childhood home I left was not in this neighborhood.

After a few quick turns, I was on the Anderson's street. Up ahead their front porch light beamed like a beacon, urging Mike to come home.

Come home.

It was eight o'clock and despair lingered, threatening to swallow me in its tidal wave. I had made it through a string of holidays without him, just me as a pretender—a poser acting as if I were a part of his family. How much more could I take?

The Andersons took me in when I could no longer live with my family. Mike and I had just started dating, but that showed the extent of their goodwill. They welcomed me with arms spread so wide I almost got lost in them. It was their kindness and Mike's love that kept me from plunging off the proverbial cliff. I didn't think I could go much longer without seeing him.

Snow fell in tiny white bombs on the windshield, melting into water almost immediately. As I came upon the Anderson's home I kept my eyes straight ahead, refusing to look at the driveway, ignoring my fear that he wasn't home, wasn't coming home. When the house loomed to my right, I had no other choice but to turn. My heart plummeted, confirming my fears. Mike's car wasn't in the driveway.

Wasn't in the driveway *yet*, I told myself and pinched my thigh.

The empty space was like a giant, gaping hole, not only in the driveway, but also in my life. This driveway needed his car in it. Didn't he realize that?

As I shuffled toward the house my cheeks stung from the cold, and my nose started to run. I tried to hurry inside toward the warmth and away from the empty space that mocked me. Except I couldn't. The path was icy. I managed an ungraceful attempt to stay on my feet until I couldn't hold on any longer, and I landed on my knees. Pain shot through my thighs; I tasted blood from where I bit my tongue.

"Dammit!" I tried to stand, slipped again, and finally managed to find my feet. Levi, my dog, was barking inside. His chocolate eyes watched me from the window where he stood on his hind legs, front paws on the sill. I tried to wave but I couldn't, my arm too stiff. Snowflakes melted into my long hair and eyelashes.

Levi pawed at the window, barking. The Andersons would be awake, but I was always afraid my animals—Levi and my cat, Scout—were too much of a nuisance, an inconvenience. I tried not to dwell on the inconvenience of *me*.

I used my key to let myself in, but I didn't need it. The Andersons hadn't locked the door. They would be willing Mike to walk through it as strongly as I was.

"Hi, Rowan. How was your day?" Mrs. Anderson, Mike's mom, clacked into the foyer on her nude pumps. She was dressed in her comfortable clothes, which for her meant pressed khaki slacks and a sweater set. She didn't wear pearls although they would have fit right in with the outfit. Her brown hair was perfectly styled, her makeup lightly applied.

Behind her, light from two table lamps cast a warm glow to the room. A fire roared in the large fireplace, the flames reflecting off the silver-framed family pictures that sat on the mantle.

I swallowed, trying to moisten my throat so my voice would sound less strained than it actually was. "Hi, Mrs. A. My day was good. A dog got adopted, the one with the broken leg that healed funny. We weren't sure anyone would take her." Levi, all eighty pounds of him, sat by my leg licking my hand. I stroked the top of his brown head and forced a smile that I knew he wouldn't believe.

"Well, that's good." She glanced out the window, lifting to her toes. Like that would help. Not seeing what she wanted, she turned back to me. "You look cold." However, she was the one rubbing her arms.

I took off my wet coat and the snow boots Mrs. Anderson gave me when we had the first big snow of the season. They were her old pair and a little big on me but warm. "It's snowing pretty hard. And the roads are getting slick."

She sighed and smoothed the sides of her hair. "I wish he would get home. I don't like him driving in this weather."

She frowned. The Andersons had four children, but Mike was their youngest and it was obvious they missed him. I understood their feelings completely.

"Has he called?" My breath caught in my throat, threatening to stay stuck if the answer was the wrong one.

"No. I just checked the home phone and my cell." Her eyes fell on me. "Did he call you?" She folded her arms. "You did take your phone today, didn't you?"

I set my wet boots out of the way and avoided her stare. She wasn't comfortable with me not carrying my phone. I couldn't tell her that the number of times I checked my phone, yearning for Mike to call or text, bordered on obsessive. It was making me crazy always seeing the blank screen, listening for a ring that wasn't coming. So I left it home to avoid the sinking feeling that came each time it didn't do what I wanted.

I shook my head. "No. I didn't take it."

"Oh, Rowan. I wish you would." She turned back to the window. "It worries me to think you can't be reached."

I put my coat in the closet. "I'm going to run upstairs and shower. I'll check my phone and if he's called, I'll let you know."

She nodded. Levi followed me as I hobbled up the stairs, my knees aching from the fall. There was a pain in my chest, too, although it was entirely unrelated to the slippery ice outside.

My phone sat on the nightstand by the bed where I slept. This room was their daughter's, Tabitha, but she left home years ago. And now, after her company offered her a position in Australia, she'd taken the job and moved far away. That meant that the Andersons never saw her and the room had become mine.

There was no message on my phone so I padded down the hall to the bathroom that I shared with Mike when he was home. Many of his things were still here—his toothbrush in the holder, his hair gel under the sink, his razor in the medicine cabinet. The only thing missing was him.

Soon steam filled the small space, a thick fog masking the reflection in the mirror. I ran the heel of my hand over the smooth surface, creating a clear oval where my face could stare back at me.

It was a face that had changed since I moved in. My gray eyes had grown brighter, my long brown hair shinier. Within a month of leaving my childhood home, I had gained eight much-needed pounds, becoming the healthiest version of myself that had ever existed.

Now, though, the face in the mirror was starting to show the same prominent cheekbones and dark circles that I had before. It was hard living in Mike's home without him here. I missed him so much I was literally fading away.

In the shower the water scalded my skin. I didn't change the temperature and took longer than necessary on purpose. Even if Mike showed up in the next five minutes, his parents would want to see him. I didn't want to interrupt their time together.

I shampooed and conditioned my hair, trying to wash out the stench of the shelter, then ran a prickly loofah over my skin, careful of my left arm where a dozen ugly lines and a very prominent *A* covered the inside, evidence of why I lived with the Andersons and not with my own family. The cuts, forged by the steel of a razor blade, were healed well enough, but old habits died hard. I was so used to not touching that arm that avoiding it was automatic, like brushing my teeth before bed.

When I walked down the hall back to my room, I listened for voices. At first, it was quiet. *Not again.* I felt so low I wasn't sure I could handle another disappointment. *How could he not come home again?* Then I heard it. Mike's voice. My breath stopped for a second as I listened.

I hurried to the window at the end of the hall that looked over the front yard and the driveway. The empty space was filled with Mike's blue Mazda.

He was home.

Mike was home.

I yanked a brush through my hair, pulled on yoga pants and a warm sweatshirt. I darted out of my bedroom and then tried to take slow, deliberate steps. I didn't want to go flying into the room like a maniacal squirrel. And I wanted him to have some time with his parents.

But the harder I tried, the faster my feet moved until I was hurdling down the stairs, soaring through the front hall, and catapulting myself into Mike's arms. He tried to catch his balance but fell onto the couch with me on top of him.

He laughed and my heart swelled. "Rowan. Oh my God. It's so good to see you."

I inhaled deeply, pulling his scent into my body. He smelled the same as I remembered; so uniquely *Mike*—musky with a hint of his hair gel—that I thought I had died and gone to Heaven. A drowning man didn't clutch a life preserver as hard as I held onto Mike.

Finally, I released my grasp so I could look at him. Stubble darker and thicker than I remembered covered his face. There were circles under his eyes, and his skin was pale.

"You look tired," I said. What I didn't tell him was that he was still the most handsome guy I had ever seen.

"God, I'm exhausted." He shimmied out from underneath me. His parents sat in opposite chairs. Mrs. Anderson's face lit brighter than a bulb, and Mr. Anderson's splashed with a look of contentment I hadn't seen in months.

Delilah, Mike's bulldog, struggled up onto his lap. "Hey girl." She licked his face and Mike laughed. The sound had been absent so long from the house that his parents and I sighed at the same time. The three of us relaxed and our smiles grew. *He was home.*

Mike put his arm around my shoulders, and I scooted into his body, wanting it to absorb my own. Delilah flashed me a look with her droopy brown eyes that told me that Mike was *her* territory, but I didn't care. She was all wrinkled fur and heavy chest and tenderness beneath the gruff exterior. Levi licked his knee, and Mike rubbed his chin.

"I'll get you something to eat." Mrs. Anderson hopped up from the chair and started toward the kitchen. "I made dinner and it's warming in the oven. Chili. Your favorite."

"I'm not hungry, Mom. I stopped on the way home."

"Well, you need to eat. You look like you're getting too skinny."

Mike patted his flat, hard stomach. He not only didn't look skinny, he looked bigger—more muscular and fit. I ran my hand over his thigh, feeling the strength that got him a position on his college soccer team, careful not to run my hand too high in front of his dad. He glanced down at me and winked.

"How was the tournament?" Mr. Anderson sat back in the chair and crossed one leg over the other.

"Oh, man. It was great! We won with only thirty seconds to go. It was amazing."

"Who scored the last goal?" Mr. Anderson rested his chin on his fingers.

Mike was quiet, and I glanced up. His pine-colored eyes sparkled in the dim light of the living room. His mouth formed into one of the biggest grins I had ever seen. "I did."

"Son, that's great!" Mr. Anderson swatted Mike's knee.

"What's great?" Mrs. Anderson returned carrying a tray filled with a pitcher of water, cups, a plate of cheese and crackers, and a bowl of chili.

"Mike scored the winning goal in the tournament," Mr. Anderson said.

"Sweetheart! I can't believe we missed that!"

"Well…" His arm tightened around my shoulders. "Maybe you can come to the next game."

"When is it?" Mr. Anderson asked, his eyes earnest. They hadn't been able to attend as many soccer games as they wanted. With Mr. Anderson's dental practice and Mrs. Anderson's church obligations, the weekends were often filled weeks in advance. Plus they *did* have someone else living in their home. It wasn't as if they were on their own.

Mike's jaw clenched, a hint that I wouldn't like the next words that came from his mouth.

"In two days."

"In two days?" Mrs. Anderson poured the water then sat down in a chair, her bright eyes dancing in the firelight. "Where? A home game?"

"Yep."

"A home tournament?" Mrs. Anderson clapped her hands. "In two days?"

He nodded.

Mrs. Anderson looked at her husband. "With the holidays over, I can get away. How about you? You're due for a little vacation. Honey, let's go!" She scooted to the edge of the seat, her knees bouncing up and down.

Mr. Anderson pulled out his phone to check his calendar. "Sure. I need to rearrange a few things, but I think we can make it work." He tossed the phone on the side table. "I'll call Danielle tomorrow and see if she can reschedule some appointments."

Mike looked at me. "What about you, Rowan? Can you come? I'd love for you to see one of the games." He squeezed my shoulder.

I hadn't watched Mike play since he went to college. With school—I was a senior this year—and work at the animal shelter, my life was busy. It made getting away on the weekends difficult, especially since Janie had started giving me more hours and more responsibility. And this tournament in two days…well, I couldn't make that either. "School starts Monday."

"Already?" He snorted. "Christmas break is over already?"

I nodded, blinking to prevent moisture from building behind my eyes.

"Wow. You forget how little time you get off in high school. I bet you can't wait until college."

If he felt my sadness cast a gray haze over the moment, he didn't react. Levi did, though, and leaned against my calves. Levi always knew when my heart was hurting. He was special like that.

"Oh, shoot. That's right." Mrs. Anderson peered at me over the top of her reading glasses. "I forgot all about that. I don't think we should leave you here alone."

The carpet's woven tan pattern suddenly became very interesting. The last months without Mike here had been awkward and at times overwhelmingly uncomfortable. They were not my parents. They should be empty nesters, and if it weren't for me, they would be. The lump in my throat throbbed.

"I'm sure she'll be okay. You're eighteen, right?" Mr. Anderson winked at me. "You might like a little alone time. You could have the house all to yourself."

There was no malice in his words, his expression. No secret yearning to get away from me. Only a desire to see his son play soccer and possibly appease me in one swift motion.

Except it didn't appease me. It made me feel inconvenient, inconsequential, and in the way.

Mike stood. "Let's talk about it later." He pulled me up by the hand. "I'm beat. I want to talk to Rowan a couple of minutes then I'm heading to bed."

Mrs. Anderson stood. "Okay, sweetheart. I'll see you in the morning." She lifted to her toes to kiss him on the cheek. Then she put her hands on my shoulders and kissed my cheek, too.

"Good night, Dad."

Mr. Anderson didn't get up. "Okay, son. See you in the morning. Hey, how about we meet up with your old coach? He sent me a text earlier asking when you'd be in town."

"Sure."

I was glad Mike pulled me out of the room because if he didn't, I wouldn't have had the strength to make my legs move. Not only were my muscles exhausted from being on my feet all day at the shelter, but the thought of him leaving in just two days made everything inside of me turn to stone.

Leaving in two days, spending half of tomorrow with his dad and old coach? He'd also want to see his friends. Spend a few minutes with his mom. *Poof!* His time here was over. I bit my lip hard but forced my jaws to unclench before I tasted blood. I would *not* be one of those needy girlfriends.

At the top of the stairs, Mike dropped his bag with a thud and turned toward me. Before I could open my mouth and release excited, encouraging words that I in no way felt, he pulled me to him.

His lips were softer, warmer than I remembered. The stubble was rough against my skin. I'd grown so used to not kissing him that it felt like I was kissing him for the first time all over again. My heart erupted into manic beats. My fingers shook from the tips down through my palm and up through my arms, a wave of electricity shooting through my blood.

When his lips parted, mine followed and everything else evaporated. At least for the next hour.

chapter two

LATER THAT night, long after his parents went to bed and the house fell into silence, Mike slipped into bed beside me. His body was hot, almost burning—solid, familiar, yet strange at the same time.

The room was dark, and I had been asleep with Scout snuggled on the pillow beside my head. When Mike lay down she jumped to the floor, still familiar with our routine. Before Mike left for college in August, we'd perfected how to carve out time together while living in his parents' home. We went to separate rooms at the end of the night, but he would sneak into bed with me later.

The alarm on my phone had two settings: one for school and one for the nights Mike came in. That setting was for four o'clock in the morning so there was little chance he would be caught tiptoeing back to his room. Guilt nipped at my conscience over sneaking around, but the need to be close to Mike far outweighed it.

I threw an arm and leg over him, feeling like I was lost in a perfect dream of sunshine and roses and sweet-perfumed air. "I've missed you," I whispered.

He folded me into his arms, and I was suddenly wide-awake in every possible way. "I missed you, too," he said, his breath warming my hair.

Those were the last words we spoke that night.

I DIDN'T wake up when Mike left my room. But when the front door slammed, reverberating throughout the house like a shock wave, I jolted upright, disoriented, and confused. Scout was back on the pillow beside me, and the rest of the bed was empty. I ran my hand over the cool sheets where Mike's warm body had lain.

The clock on my nightstand read eight o'clock. That must've been Mike leaving with his dad to meet his high school soccer coach. Or it was Mrs. Anderson going to the grocery store and then heading to church to see if there was anything to do. The morning spanned out in front of me like a giant, empty abyss.

I grabbed my cell phone and flipped it open. There were two texts waiting for me.

The first one was from my grandmother.

Won't you come by for dinner? I miss you.

I deleted that one. A remote part of me, in a very deep, obsolete place in my heart, felt a flash of tenderness that she still tried so hard to reenter my life. Since May, I rarely answered her texts or calls, and her attempts to see me went unfulfilled. I wasn't ready to move on, wasn't ready to forgive.

The next text was from my best friend, Jess.

Meet me at the diner. I'm starving.

Jess and I had been best friends since the ninth grade when we met in a physical education class. She lived in an apartment in town with her alcoholic father who preferred the bottle and an endless string of girlfriends over his daughter.

I sent her a text that I'd meet her in twenty minutes and got dressed. With a ponytail holding my long hair back, I dug around in the drawers for a pair of designer jeans Tabitha had left me and a long-sleeved T-shirt. These shirts had been my wardrobe staple for years, ever since the first time I cut my skin with a razor blade.

I wrapped a black scarf around my neck and inserted the tiny gold hoop earrings Mike gave me months ago. It was the only jewelry I wore; the only jewelry I owned except for an old, worn-out watch with a black leather band that was cracked and dry.

For the first time since summer, I had to put a belt around my waist to keep the jeans from sagging down my butt. Whether or not I was hungry, I would make myself eat breakfast today. At least a hard-boiled egg. Maybe a few bites of oatmeal. A glass of juice.

After I dumped food in Scout's bowl, I ran downstairs. The house was quiet except for Delilah's gruff snores coming from the couch. Levi got up when he saw me. I let him out into the yard as I shimmied into a pair of black leather boots—another hand-me-down from Tabitha. When he came back inside I wiped his wet feet on a towel I kept in the closet, careful to make sure they were clean, and pulled the door shut.

There were only two restaurants in our small, rural town—a pizza restaurant called Mario's and a diner simply called Diner.

I pulled into a parking space and fed coins into the meter. The front of the diner had two huge windows that allowed passersby to see every single person inside. It certainly wasn't a place to go for privacy, but in a small town like this, privacy didn't really exist.

I could see Jess through the windows. She was bent over a large soda, chewing on the end of the straw as she gazed toward the far wall. Over the summer, she had cut her hair into choppy layers that fell to her chin and changed the color from cherry red to ink-black—a perfect match for her somber wardrobe.

"Don't look so morose." I slid onto the opposite bench.

"Hey, Ro." Her voice was flat and toneless.

"Um, did your dog just die?"

She rolled her eyes and took a sip of soda. "I can't take care of myself, much less a dog."

The brown liquid shot up through the clear straw then back down. Up. Down. Up. Down. It was like watching a ride at a carnival.

"Are you okay?" Against the shabby green leather of the seat, Jess stood out like a gothic statue in a valley of evergreens. She was dressed head to toe in black—black skirt, black off-the-shoulder sweater, black combat boots. Her eyes were rimmed in heavy-black liner, thick even behind the tortoise-shelled glasses that covered half her face. The new tattoo, a scorpion on the inside of her wrist, was also black.

"Tell me your dad hasn't seen that tattoo. He's not going to be happy." I yanked the straw out of her mouth.

"His head is so far up Carol's ass he doesn't notice when I come or go. Although he does notice when the wine rack is empty or the laundry hasn't been done."

I didn't respond. What was there to say to that?

"Mr. Sumners doesn't like it, though. He says I'm too young to have a tattoo. He got really mad, actually. Got all, like, *'You need to be eighteen to get a tattoo. Did you forge your father's signature? I'm going to call him myself.'*" Mr. Sumners was Jess' boss at the used bookstore where she worked.

"He won't, will he? Call your dad?"

She snorted as the waitress, a girl named Chelsea who graduated with Mike last year, came up on silent feet. "I'll have another Coke. No ice." Jess didn't give her so much as a glance.

"I'll have orange juice. Thanks." Chelsea walked away with a bored look on her plain face.

"Nah. He won't call my dad. He doesn't like him. I think he's trying to assume the," she crooked her fingers, "father figure role. It's not gonna happen, though."

Mr. Sumners was the closest thing to a father figure Jess had. She pretended that his overbearing concern bothered her, but I think she secretly liked it.

"I take it he doesn't know about Paul."

She snorted and opened a packet of sugar, dumping the contents onto her pink tongue. Paul and Jess had started dating last school year. They had to keep their relationship quiet because not only was he several years older than her—she was seventeen and he was around his mid-twenties—but he also used to be a substitute art teacher at our school.

The waitress brought the drinks and flipped to a clean sheet of paper in a tiny notebook. "Do you want to order?"

"I'll have eggs. A really big plate of eggs." Jess opened her hands in a wide oval. "Extra eggs. And bacon. Throw some toast in there, too. Maybe a muffin if you have them." Jess pushed her glasses up her nose, dumped another packet of sugar in her mouth, and then dumped the next one on the table.

"Oatmeal or something." I waved my hand in the air. "Jess, that's *a lot* of food."

"Yeah." She took a long drink.

Her roots were starting to show, blaringly blonde against the dyed strands.

"Your roots are showing. I know you told me you have blonde hair but I've never seen it. What's going on?"

Jess' blue eyes, bloodshot and sunken, flashed at me. She pulled off her glasses, and I saw just how dark the circles were underneath.

"Nothing. I'm just tired." She pulled at a strand of hair until it came out between her fingertips. She threw it onto the floor and picked at another.

"You're lying."

She shrugged. "Did Mike make it back last night?"

I watched her for a minute then sighed. "Yeah. He's back. Finally. Got in late last night. Get this, though. He has a tournament, so he's leaving again…tomorrow."

"What? You're kidding, right?"

I fiddled with Jess' discarded sugar wrappers.

"He just got home. And when was the last time you saw him? It seems like forever."

"Like I don't know that," I snapped. Her eyes widened. "I'm sorry. I mean, no, I haven't seen him in…well, forever. Like once since he left in August."

Jess watched me as she took another long sip. "That really sucks," she said with the straw hanging out of her mouth.

"I know." I folded a wrapper into a tiny airplane. It did suck. Big time. What good was having a boyfriend if I never saw him? And what was I still doing living in his house without him there? "His parents are going up for the game. They asked if I wanted to go. But I can't."

"Why not?"

The bells that hung from the main door chimed loudly. Without thinking, I whipped around as I shot out a quick prayer that it was Mike coming to find me, to squeeze in as much time together as possible. But it wasn't. I turned and tried not to let my shoulders slump too low. It was just an elderly woman I recognized from church. She shuffled to a table one row over.

I forced my mind to refocus. "Did you forget that school starts Monday?"

She rolled her eyes. "Whatever. I may not finish the year. I mean, who needs a diploma? It's a joke. It's not like you can get a job or anything even if you have graduated."

"Yeah, then you can pump gas for the rest of your life."

Chelsea set a plate in front of Jess with a clang followed by two smaller plates. Jess grabbed her fork and shoved a mountain-sized bite into her mouth. Chelsea placed a steaming bowl of oatmeal in front of me. I filled a spoon and blew on the hot surface.

"I'm not pumping no one's gas." Jess' mouth was full of food as she talked. "Paul will find a job and he can work. I'll stay home."

"And do what?" I sputtered. "You're kidding me, right?"

Her eyes, as cool as ice, looked up at me.

"Jess? What's going on?" I slammed my hands on the table, ready to demand an answer when someone squealed my name. It wasn't the deep voice I dreamed it would be. Instead, it was my sister. Trina darted through the door, sending the bells into a frenzy.

"Rowan!" she squealed again, as if the first time she said my name wasn't enough. She bounced toward us, her face lit up with teeth and lipstick, and bright splashes of blush.

Her blonde ponytail flapped behind her like a windshield wiper as her hips swayed in a way no sixteen-year-old's should. I slouched down into the booth. My sister was the last person I wanted to see.

Why?

Because I hated her.

"Hi, Ro!" Trina plopped onto the bench beside me, pushing against my hip until I scooted over. "And Jess, I haven't seen you in forever!"

Jess' stare was colder than the ice they'd put in her drink even though she'd asked them to leave it out. "What do you want?" Jess spat.

Trina pushed her lip out. "I just want to say *hi*. Jeez, Jess. Grumpy much?" Trina turned in the seat to face me. "So. Guess what?" Her blue eyes were full of fireworks—pretty on the outside, thrilling even, but with an underlying ability to set fire to anything they wanted. I wrapped my arms around my stomach. If I could've slid between those dingy bench cushions and disappeared, I would have.

My sister was not someone to trust. She was a lying, manipulative, psychotic bitch. In other words, she was just like our mother. Last year Trina had accused Mike of getting her pregnant. When she realized no one believed her, she accused him of rape. No, Trina was not someone to be trusted.

Jess stopped eating and flipped her head between me and my sister as if it were on a pivot. Trina's perfume was too strong. The rose scent burned my throat and made me cough.

"You're never going to believe this," she continued, giving me a hard smack on the back. I resisted the urge to punch her. "I mean, it's the most amazing news ever."

I braced myself for the avalanche that was coming.

"Dad's back." Her lips parted to flash perfectly straight teeth smudged with lipstick.

Dad's back. Dread washed over me like a cold rain and threatened to drown me, to consume me faster than a starving, ferocious tiger could consume a terrified rabbit.

chapter three

JESS' EXPRESSION was a mirror image of my own—full of disbelief, confusion, *fear*. My dad was back.

Last year, my dad had used my face as a punching bag when he found out Trina was pregnant. It didn't matter that she was the one who'd gotten knocked up, not me. But ever since my baby brother, Aidan, died when I was ten, I had been the one to blame for anything bad that happened to our family—including his death. It wasn't until last spring that we discovered my mom had killed him. By then it was too late. Years of being blamed for everything had left its mark—inside and out.

I hadn't seen my dad in months. He hadn't called. Hadn't texted. Hadn't popped up at the Anderson's to wish his eldest daughter a happy eighteenth birthday.

"What do you mean your *Dad's back*?" Red fireballs flew from Jess' eyes and shaped her words into little, short bursts. I was glad she was speaking because words weren't forming in my brain or my mouth. Instead, panic was racing through my body as if I were plummeting off a building.

Trina nodded, her hair flopping up and down. If she clapped her hands and danced a jig, she couldn't have been more excited. "Can you believe it? He's back!"

"Yes," spat Jess, "I heard that part. But *what* does he want?" She pushed away her plate of food.

I stared into the oatmeal, my thoughts more useless than the bowl of mush sitting in front of me.

"I don't know," she chirped. "He showed up last night. You know, it was just me and Gran at home." She waved her hand in the air. Trina and my mom's mom, Gran, lived in my childhood home together. My mom was in jail for the murder of my baby brother. It had turned out that Dad's resentment toward me for killing his son was misplaced.

My mother had killed him and let me take the blame. It had been months since I'd seen either of my parents. I rarely saw Gran and tried to avoid Trina. And now my sister was saying Dad was back?

Trina's fingers, hot and moist, grazed my hand. Her long nails were painted hot pink. "He wants to see you, Ro. I think he's sorry for, well, you know, everything. He asked me where you were staying."

I yanked my hand away.

"You didn't tell him, did you?" Jess demanded. "It's none of his damned business."

"God, Jess. Take a pill." She snarled her lip then turned back to me. "Can't we go somewhere else and talk? You know, *alone*?"

My senses came whooshing back to me with the ferocity of gale force winds. "No!" My voice was so loud it echoed off the tiled walls. The elderly woman sitting nearby peered at me from behind thick glasses. "No. You and I do not need to talk alone. And I don't need to see Dad. Don't tell him where I am. Don't encourage him to call me, see me, nothing. I have a new family and that's that."

Even as I said those last words I knew they weren't true. The Andersons weren't my family. But neither were Trina, Gran, Mom, and Dad. I was really without anyone. A sort of eighteen-year-old orphan.

I sat on my hands to keep from shoving her out of the booth. "Don't you have somewhere to be?" I narrowed my eyes, willing imaginary knives to shoot out of them.

Her mouth fell open. Her head kept flipping back and forth between me and Jess in disbelief. Since I had moved out of the house, I went to great lengths to avoid Trina. She was as dangerous as a pit bull puppy—cute on the outside, deadly on the inside. I didn't answer her texts or return her calls even though she and Gran both contacted me at least once a week. There was nothing between us. When your sister accuses your boyfriend of rape and getting her pregnant, and your Gran knows you didn't kill your baby brother but lets you take the blame anyway, there were really no ties left.

"You're such a bitch, Ro. God. I just wanted to come and see you. Maybe try to work things out. If Dad is back to stay, you could come home. We could be a family again."

An ugly guffaw burst out of my mouth. "You do realize our mom is in jail for the murder of our baby brother?"

She shrugged and for the first time since she sat down I saw a crack in her chipper façade.

"Well…" She pulled a napkin between her fingers and started shredding it. "I mean, why not? She'll be given parole sometime, I'm sure. We can be there waiting for her."

I would never go back to that home. Never. I would never return to that family. Ever. I'd be a homeless bum begging for loose change on the streets of New York City before I returned there.

I whipped my hands from under my thighs, rage coloring my vision red, and shoved her. Hard. She fell off the bench and onto the floor. The elderly lady gasped and threw a hand over her mouth.

"Ouch!" Trina's cheeks reddened.

"Get out of here, and don't mention being a family again." I scooted to the edge of the bench, clenching my fists. "Not now. Not ever. Got it?"

"Rowan." Trina scrambled to her feet and threw her hands on her hips. "You can't deny who you are or where you came from.

You're a Slone, like it or not. Your mom is a murderer and your father is a bully. But they're part of you. You'll never escape where you came from."

I lunged at her, but she jumped back. "Get out!" I shouted.

We stared at each other, neither blinking, until she finally huffed and turned. She walked past Chelsea who looked like this was the most excitement she'd seen in weeks. She threw open the door sending the bells clanging, walked out of the diner, and down the sidewalk. It wasn't until she passed out of view that I slumped down in the seat, my body numb and shaking at the same time.

Jess said nothing. I said nothing. After a few quiet moments, she pulled her plate over and took a huge bite of the eggs. They had to be cold by now, but she didn't seem to mind.

"I don't know what to say," she confessed between mouthfuls of food. "I wish she would just disappear."

Watching her shovel food into her mouth was a welcome respite from the thoughts in my head and the turmoil inside me. "I don't know what to say either. I'm not sure what to think."

After she polished off the eggs, she grabbed the muffin and ripped the paper off, shoving a huge piece in her mouth. Her red lipstick had long since come off and her lips were pale, almost white with the loss of color.

"I don't like this," she stated.

"I know." I sighed. "I wonder why he's back?" My question trailed off into a whisper as Jess used the side of her fork to scrape food off the plate.

My dad was a hard man. He'd spent years in the Army, more years as a prison guard, and even more years than that hating my mother. He hated me and Trina, too. Dad didn't want to marry Mom, but she'd gotten pregnant in high school. He had resented us all ever since.

My childhood was shaped by images of heavy black boots, pressed gray uniforms, and accusing, stern eyes that followed me with thinly veiled resentment—if they bothered to look at me at all.

Jack Slone did not love us. Trina was delusional to think he'd come back for any good reason. Maybe he came back to kill us like my mom had killed Aidan.

I shuddered and turned in the booth to look out the windows, expecting a tall, straight-backed, dark-haired man to walk by. What would I do if he did? Run? Stay and fight? Was there a chance he wanted to make amends?

But the sidewalk stayed empty and I turned back to Jess, suddenly exhausted. My mind felt like a painting, all reds, oranges, blacks, and browns that had a bucket of water dumped over it. My thoughts were the streams of paint that flowed down the wall, misshapen, uneven, ugly.

Jess began eating my oatmeal. The only words that took root in the image of the painting massacre were, "You're acting really weird."

"I'm just hungry." She took a gulp of soda.

Several seconds passed as she shoveled food into her mouth. "I don't want to think about—" I cleared my throat. "*Her* right now. Or him. I need a distraction. So spill it."

"I'm pregnant."

Well, there you have it.

"YOU'RE PREGNANT?"

She spooned the rest of the oatmeal into her mouth. "I know. I can't believe it either." Little crumbs from the muffin peppered her lips.

"You're pregnant?"

"Yup. Knocked up. Bun in the oven." She chewed a piece of the ice she hadn't wanted. "Preggers." She went through every phrase she could think of: "Pickle-eating freak show. Waddling duck mama." She clapped really loud and squealed. "Here's a good one! Is that a baby in there or are you just happy to see me?"

"That's not funny. At least not that last one." I took a deep breath and refocused. "Are you sure? I mean, how?"

"Come on, Ro. You're smart. You know how these things work."

"Don't be a smartass. Did you not think to use, you know, *something*?"

She picked up a piece of toast, and took several seconds to swipe a large glob of butter over the top and followed that with strawberry jam. "I took one of those tests you pee on. Got it all over my hand."

"You didn't answer my question."

"It was pretty disgusting." I didn't point out that the question remained unanswered. Clearly, the answer was obvious. "The test said that I'm pregnant. I need to go to the clinic next week and I guess, you know, have someone confirm it. Or something. You'll come with me won't you?"

She didn't have to ask. Of course I would go with her.

"Is that why your roots are showing when I've never seen them before?" Jess' hair had been blue, red, black, and even rainbow-hued for Prom last year. But I'd never seen it blonde.

"Yeah. Well, I guess so. I mean, I was watching some show the other day, even before I found out about, well, *this*." She motioned toward her stomach. "And it talked about all the things that could harm a baby. Hair dye is one of them."

Hair dye? What about being a teenage mom? Brochures covered an entire shelf in my guidance counselor's office at school with pictures of smiling, content teens and enormous, swollen bellies.

"So you're going to keep it?"

"Yeah, sure. Why not?" She finally fell back against the seat, shoving the fork to the side. "I mean, Paul and I will raise it together. You know. Be a family."

For the next hour, I didn't think of Mike, Trina, or my dad. I thought about Jess and that life was a holy mess.

JESS HAD to get to work after we left the diner. We walked the few blocks down to the bookstore. It had a brick façade with one large window that in no way added light to the musty, dark interior.

She hugged me tight. "Call ya later," she said over her shoulder as she walked away.

"'Kay," I answered. Her boots pounded against the broken concrete as she moved toward the door. What would she look like with a swollen stomach? With a baby? I couldn't stop the frown that spread across my face. And since she turned around right before she walked into the bookstore, I couldn't hide it.

After Jess went inside, I checked my watch. It was noon and I hadn't heard from Mike, but hopefully he was back home. I hurried to my car, pushing Jess' problems and my own to the back of my mind. If there was one thing that would brighten this day it was seeing Mike.

The closer I got to the Anderson's the more butterflies beat a steady rhythm in my chest—like they did every time I saw him. He stood several inches taller than me and had dark, short hair with gorgeous green eyes surrounded by thick, black lashes.

It had taken awhile for me to let him get close, to let him love me. Coming from a past like mine had left me with a lot of baggage—physical and emotional scars. But he had managed to make me feel loved like no one else ever had. For the first time in my life, someone made me feel special.

When I pulled into the Anderson's driveway and saw his car, a smile spread across my face so bright it warmed my heavy heart. I was able to push the morning's events to the back of my mind and focus on seeing Mike and spending the rest of the day with him. I hadn't seen him that morning and he was leaving tomorrow, but we'd have the afternoon and that would be enough. Anything was enough. I skipped toward the house, avoiding any patches of ice.

When I walked in, I was hit with a blast of male voices. Mike's friends from his high school soccer team were over. I hadn't spent a lot of time with them, but enough to know their voices. Mike must've picked them up while he was out. Of course they would be home from college, too. I stopped in the foyer and shut the door with a soft *click*.

Snow from my boots was melting into brown water on the rug. I bit my lip to keep from pouting. Would I have any time with Mike other than in the middle of the night? And when I thought of him leaving *tomorrow*, I wanted to cry.

I yanked off my boots and fell back against the door. Levi rose to his feet and padded over to me. He sat on his haunches, his head level with my hip. He wouldn't move until he knew I was okay. But as I leaned there, I wasn't sure how long that would take.

Was this it? my mind screamed. *Is this all I had? Living with a family that was not my own. Hating the family I had. Having a boyfriend I never got to see. A father who may or may not be back to finish the job? Was this it?*

I darted up the stairs and slid into my bedroom without making any noise. Scout meowed and ran her soft head over my cheek when I lay down on the bed.

Tears were not welcome, but my heart hurt. My fingers shook, itched for *something*. I hadn't cut since the day I moved in with the Andersons, and I didn't plan to start now. But the desire was so strong I could taste it, almost like I was sucking on the cool steel of a razor blade.

After several long, slow inhales, followed by long, slow exhales, the shaking in my fingers subsided enough. I opened the drawer on the nightstand and pulled out a journal Mrs. Anderson gave me for Christmas. I hadn't had it long, but it was proving to be a distraction for my restless yearning.

The journal was made of distressed brown leather with a smooth, blank cover except for the bottom right corner where my name was engraved. I turned to a new sheet of paper that was blaringly white in its emptiness. I laid the point of the pen against the pristine surface, creating a small black dot. Then I wrote.

> *My outside is smooth,*
> *With only a glimpse of pain.*
> *But underneath,*
> *I am raw.*
> *Terrified,*
> *Streaming crimson tears.*
> *Where will I go from here?*
> *With all my fears…*
> *Fears…*
> *Fears…*

I stopped before I wrote the word *fears* again. If I allowed myself, I would fill the entire journal with that loaded word until it consumed every page.

Why couldn't I just walk into Mike's house and go sit with him and his friends? Why did I have to pout and run away before anyone could see me? Why did I have to have the parents I did? The family I did?

I tossed the journal back into the drawer and went to the mirror that hung on the wall behind the dresser. I pulled the ponytail holder from my hair and let my hair fall around my shoulders in a brown curtain. My skin was pale and I pinched my cheeks to make them pink then bit my lips and watched them redden. I pulled out a gray sweater to help cover the looseness of my clothes.

Go downstairs, Rowan. Join the group. More laughter burst through the silence, wafting up the stairs. *Be a part of something for once.*

I ran a brush through my hair. Just as I resolved to go downstairs, the front door slammed with a loud bang. It must be his parents leaving.

When I looked out the window at the end of the hallway, I saw Mike walking past my car and going to the driver's seat of his car.

He got in and his friends piled in around him. Without so much as a glance back at the house, or at my car, Mike pulled out of the driveway. Right behind him were his parents, pulling away in their sedan.

I went downstairs, Scout on my heels, to make sure the dogs at least were still here. Scout hopped onto the back of a chair and stared out the window. Levi watched me from the couch where he lay near a snoring Delilah. On the side table was a note in Mike's scratchy handwriting. *We went to the grocery store. Having a small party tonight. Invite Jess. 7:00. Love you.*

So this was what I got for running away. I got another dose of how it felt to be completely alone in the world.

chapter four

THE THREADS that bound my life together had always been loosely tied. Since I'd moved in with the Andersons, they'd woven tighter, helping me feel stronger. But now I could feel the threads starting to unravel until I feared I would unwind string by string, and end up like one of those old-fashioned dolls whose stitches were made of thick, black yarn. If I wasn't careful there would be nothing left, nothing but fabric, cotton stuffing, and those haunting black button eyes.

When Aidan died, I had been the one watching him. He was two months old and I was ten. Mom and Dad had gotten into another ear-splitting fight. He left. She, in her obese, lumbering walk, carried her huge body down the hall and locked the door to her bedroom. When Aidan started to cry there was no one to get him. Except me.

I had left Trina sitting on the couch, made him a bottle, changed his diaper, and rocked him until he was sleepy. When I laid him back in his crib, he cried out but then went to sleep. Because it was cold out, I put a blanket over his legs and hips.

The next morning he was dead. They said he died from SIDS—sudden infant death syndrome caused by being overheated from the blanket. What I didn't learn until last May was my mother had killed him, jealous that my father loved my brother more than her.

Aidan's death set the tone for the next seven years of my life. Guilt had settled into my bones and ate away at me day by long day. My family blamed me. I blamed me.

But I had finally broken free, as free as someone with scars like mine can be, and moved on, moved away. It wasn't me who'd killed Aidan. It was Mom. Now I was in a good place, here at the Anderson's home. So why did I feel utterly and completely alone?

Did my dad know that it was Mom who was responsible? That she had smothered him in his sleep? Would it change anything if he did know?

My heart felt heavy, like it was weighted with a ten-ton boulder. The world beneath my feet was shaking more and more each day, threatening to knock me over. I had come so far from the razor-wielding girl I was last year. But things felt like they were slipping, and I wasn't sure how much more I could take.

"I don't want to be that girl," I whispered. "I don't want to be *that girl*." The girl with all the problems. The girl who whines, cries, pleads with life to be better. I want to be the girl who survives, who finds a way to be happy, who finds her *place*.

The air inside the house was stifling, so heavy it pushed against my shoulders, shoving me down, beating me down so far until I wasn't sure that girl existed.

I hadn't cried since I'd moved in with the Andersons. It had been one thing that I wouldn't allow, couldn't allow. If I cried, it was like the beginning of a crack; like opening a door and inviting a demon in. If I cried, I wouldn't be able to stop and where would that leave me? Back on the bathroom floor with Dad's rusty razor in my hand, slicing through the pain one line at a time.

"No!" I cried. "Don't go back there. *Don't go back there.*" I rocked back and forth, trying to sooth myself like I used to soothe Aidan. "Calm down, Rowan. It's okay."

Levi pushed his large, warm body beside mine and nudged at my arm until I fell into his solid warmth. He let me snuggle until calm eased into my mind.

I grabbed my coat and left. There was only one place capable of soothing my soul, and I had to go there.

BEAUTY MOUNTAIN was where Mike and I had our first kiss last year, where our relationship had truly started. It was a high mountain peak outside of town. You could only reach it by a narrow, dirt road that wove straight up a mountainside.

It was cold but had stopped snowing. My old car sputtered and spewed and coughed, but made the climb at a slow, steady pace. There were no other cars and the thick, heavy forest blanketing either side obscured the afternoon sky.

I parked off the side of the road and hiked to our rock, a large gray boulder that fit both Mike and me perfectly. This was the place Mike and I often came when we needed more than just stolen hours in the middle of the night; when living under his parents' watchful eyes proved too much.

It felt foreign, alien, to be here without Mike. The surface of the rock was too wide for just me. If the thin crack that ran through it suddenly opened, it would swallow me whole and no one would ever know. But it was solid, cold, nearly frozen and helped ground me in my life.

Dad.
Trina.
Jess.
Mike.
Gran.
Mom…

My breath came out in a wave of white mist and the skin on my cheeks felt feverish, hot. The surface of the rock was smooth and I lay down on my stomach, sprawling across its wide surface. The feel of the frigid stone helped soothe the ache that lingered inside me.

My eyes closed as my lungs filled with the musty, earthy smell. The trees, leaves long gone, created a haunting canopy over my head. I pulled my sleeves over my hands, curling the seams into balled fists.

There is no razor. There is only me. My fingertips tingled, but I focused on deep breaths—in and out; in and out—and I willed the world away.

"RO, WAKE up. Rowan?" Someone shook my shoulder. "Rowan!"

I blinked and lifted my head. My jaw hurt from lying on the rock. I opened and closed my mouth, pain shooting through my temple. My arms and legs, ears and fingers, nose and toes felt frozen. My body was stiff and sore, jerking painfully when Mike put his arms around me and helped me sit up.

"What are you doing here?" The day had turned to twilight around me, shadows dancing gray and pink over the distant peak.

"I'm sorry." I ran a hand over my face and worked my jaw to loosen the stiffness. "I just needed some air."

"I've been trying to call you all afternoon." He climbed onto the rock and pulled me into his lap where I fit like a small child. My arms wove around his neck and I settled into his chest, my cheek pulsing with the beat of his heart.

"Ro, what's wrong?" His breath warmed the top of my head.

Seconds passed then minutes as we gazed through the thick branches, watching the horizon darken into streaks of orange and red. My watch said it was only five o'clock, but the day had slipped out of my grasp, as had my time with Mike.

Words would ruin the moment and I wanted, *needed*, to capture this like a camera captures a perfect picture before an angry black crow swoops in at the last minute and ruins it. In Mike's arms I was safe, content like I wasn't anywhere else in the world. I drank in every minute detail, imprinting it in my mind, tucking it away for safe keeping so I could pull it up and remember it when he was hours away and I didn't know when I would see him again. His smell, the feel of his hair on my hands, the beat of his heart against my cheek. Everything was important to remember.

He tried to lean to the side and look at my face, but I clung too tightly for him to move. The threads that were loosening were slowly weaving back together. I was becoming whole again.

"WE'D BETTER get back." Mike ran his fingers through my hair, sending a tremor down my neck. We were snuggled so close together, with his coat opened in the front to allow me in, there was no separation. If I got close enough, would he be able to disentangle himself? Would he want to?

"Come on," he said. "You're shivering."

"Okay." My eyes strained to focus in the darkness. I could barely see the outline of his face, or the trees, or anything for that matter.

He jumped to the ground then lifted me down beside him and kissed me. I lifted to my toes to meet his lips full on. His arms wrapped around my waist and helped lift me higher. My hands wove into his hair, and he held me tighter. If I could get lost anywhere, it was in his kiss.

Several moments passed, the kiss threatening to turn into more. But I knew his parents were expecting him. I forced myself to break the kiss. It didn't work. Minutes passed, and I pulled away again. "Come on. We'd better go."

There would be more time tonight after everyone was asleep.

AT THE house, preparations were in place for more than just dinner with a few friends. Mounds of unpacked grocery bags were piled down one half of the black granite counter and down the other half was a line of bowls, some full of food, some empty and waiting.

"Mom, we're home."

The smell of marinating meat filled the air, and my stomach rumbled. Mrs. Anderson stood at the wide windows that overlooked the backyard, watching Mr. Anderson struggle with the grill. His curses rang all the way through the closed door. Mr. Anderson had wanted a new grill for Christmas but Mike's mom gave him new golf clubs instead. Levi was rolling in the grass behind him, unconcerned and happy.

"Hi, Mrs. A."

She turned. "Hi, you two." She wiped her hands on her *Kiss the Cook* apron and walked to the counter. "Your father is going to catch his hair on fire." She shoved two enormous salad tongs into a bowl and started tossing. A red cherry tomato popped out and rolled across the floor.

"You should've bought him a new one for Christmas," Mike teased. He stepped over the tomato and headed outside, flipping the collar up on his coat as he shut the door behind him.

Mrs. Anderson smiled, shaking the salad dressing in a well-manicured hand. "How was your day, dear?"

"It was good." I picked up the tomato and threw it into the trash. "I met Jess for lunch. Saw Mike for a while this afternoon." *Saw my sister. Heard my father was back. Jess is pregnant.*

"That's nice. I'm sure you two have a lot of catching up to do." She sighed. "I can't believe he's leaving so soon, although I'm sure you can't believe it either." She set the salad and dressing on the table and flashed me a sympathetic smile. "It's supposed to start snowing again, but I hope it doesn't. I'm excited to see Mike play in this tournament." She moved back to the counter and started slicing bread. "I know it's an indoor tournament but still. The roads could be bad."

I nodded and dumped tortilla chips into a bowl.

"The youth group at the church is having a movie night next weekend. Do you think you would like to go? You have to RSVP. They're expecting a good turnout."

An image of Mike rolling his eyes popped into my head. His parents went to church every Sunday and expected me to go with them. I hadn't grown up going to church, but if it made the Andersons happy, I did it. That didn't mean I wanted to go more often than was absolutely necessary. There was something about sitting in the pew alongside Mike's parents without him, and the eyes of the congregation firmly fixated on my back, that left a sour feeling in my stomach.

One Sunday over a month ago, I overheard Mrs. Anderson talking with a silver-haired widow after the service. The elderly woman had her wrinkled hand on Mrs. Anderson's arm: *You are so kind to take her in. God has smiled on that child by sending you as her angel. I don't know how you do it, though. She has to come with an awful lot of problems.*

Mrs. Anderson's response was: *We love Rowan, and it's a joy to have her live with us.* I fell in love with Mike's mom at that moment with a ferocity I'd never felt toward my own mother. But I also felt ashamed. She wasn't my mother. She was my boyfriend's mother.

I avoided church as much as I could after that. "I have to work. Janie has been giving me more hours."

"Animals really love you. God has certainly given you a gift. I think you've found your calling, sweetheart."

Delilah trotted in, sniffed my pants, farted, and walked away.

"Well, most animals love you." Mrs. Anderson laughed and I couldn't help but join in.

"How many people are coming tonight?" I poured salsa into a small, hand-painted bowl.

"Thirty. Maybe forty. I doubt more than that."

My back was turned so she couldn't see my disappointment. So many people? But I didn't want to seem less than a team player so I threw myself into party preparations, filling the rest of the bowls with whatever Mrs. Anderson told me to, laying out plates and napkins, utensils and cups. I lit candles to make the house smell nice and put Scout up in my room. Mike was throwing Levi's ball while he watched his dad try to get the grill to light.

I realized I had forgotten to invite Jess. I ran upstairs and grabbed my phone off the nightstand.

> Come over now. Party at Anderson's.

She texted back immediately.

> Just woke up. What?

> Party. Andersons. You. Here. Now.

> K.

I didn't tell her to invite Paul. There was a good chance Mrs. Anderson knew Paul, or at least who he was. She volunteered at the high school when Mike was a student, and Paul was a regular substitute. Best to let that relationship remain in secrecy, at least until the entire world found out he was the father of a seventeen-year-old's baby.

chapter five

MIKE'S FRIENDS were coming over at seven. Mrs. Anderson had also invited a few of her friends from church so it was going to be a full house. It was already six forty-five so I needed to hurry. I left the kitchen with a smile plastered on my face. I even whistled a few notes of some show tune I remembered from childhood.

Soon I was in my room rummaging through the closet. Between my own purchases, what Mrs. Anderson bought me, and what Tabitha had left behind, I had a completely new wardrobe: jeans, khakis, shorts, skirts, and a slew of long-sleeved shirts and sweaters. There were even piles of shoes in the back of the closet, some so barely worn they looked new.

I had transformed right before my own eyes into someone else entirely, from a tiny spit of a girl in worn-out jeans, a hoodie with the word ARMY spread across the back, and boots bought from the thrift store into a young woman with soft makeup, freshly trimmed hair, and designer jeans. Sometimes I didn't recognize myself.

I undressed, throwing my clothes onto the bed, and stood in front of the mirror. My hipbones jutted out against the white cotton underwear. If I wanted to, I could trace my rib cage and count the bones underneath. The breasts I had grown when I finally had gained some weight were dwindling back down to tiny, nearly nonexistent buds.

I sighed and watched my chest go up, then down. My stomach was churning slowly. I ran a hand over the concave surface. Hunger was something I rarely felt, so I knew it wasn't that. I sucked in my cheeks and my cheekbones protruded sharply, making my reflection ugly. With the thumb and middle finger of my right hand, I circled them around my left wrist. The tips met and then overlapped. What did Mike think of my losing weight again? Did he even notice?

I went back to the closet, pulled out a pale yellow sweater set, and tossed it on the bed. Then I grabbed a dark brown patterned skirt. Mrs. Anderson had even bought me a pair of nude pumps to match.

I held the skirt to my nose and inhaled. The last time I wore it was to Mike's cousin's wedding the weekend before Mike left for college. He kept lifting the skirt high up my knee under the table. At one point toward the end of the reception, his parents were on the dance floor and we were at the table alone. I let him push his hand all the way up. His touch had sent shockwaves through my body. Even minutes later, when his parents returned, the flush was still on my cheeks and Mrs. A. asked if I had a fever, going so far as to lay a cold hand on my forehead.

I crumpled up the skirt and threw it across the room, the wooden hanger leaving a mark on the light blue wall. I grabbed the sweater set and threw it on top of the skirt. The shoes were right inside the door of the closet. I hurled them, too.

I crawled into the closet and started throwing shoes, one at a time, across the room. Some smacked against the wall and dropped to the floor with a thud. A couple landed on the bed. A shiny black pump with a heel larger than I could maneuver went sailing toward the dresser and knocked off the lamp.

Tucked away in the farthest, dark corner of the closet were my old black boots, the only pair of shoes I wore last year. I had bought these with my first paycheck after I started working for Dan, my old boss at the used car lot.

I had cashed that check, grabbed Jess, and then hightailed it to the thrift store. These boots were beloved. But I didn't wear them anymore. I hadn't worn them since I moved in with Mike's family. They didn't go with my new, fancier clothes. Now I had a designer pair of boots that Mr. and Mrs. Anderson had given me for Christmas and a pair Tabitha left before she moved to Australia.

With the old boots tucked under my arm, I crawled out of the closet, clothes smacking into my face, and returned to the mirror. I slid my feet into the boots, the black blaring against the pale skin of my legs.

My feet filled the soft, worn leather; my toes spread out, flexing and stretching. My heel nestled into the perfect dip in the foot bed. I sifted through the other discarded shoes and found the silk skirt and sweater set. Laying them out on the bed, I smoothed the wrinkles and looked at them for a long time, my feet getting sweaty.

Without putting them on, I went back to the mirror. My skin was pale all over my body except where the scars colored the inside of my arm red. With a fingernail, I dug into the skin between my breasts and scratched a line down to my lower stomach; not breaking skin, but leaving a faint, crimson line in my nail's wake. Now there was another place on my body that wasn't perfect.

I scratched four fingernails over my chest, shoulder to shoulder. Then I ran four fingers up my thigh, starting above my knees and ending right before my hips. My torso looked like a map.

As I stared at myself, unblinking, the lines began to pulse and grow redder somehow, even though I hadn't broken skin. I thought about Mike's old razor in the bathroom. I didn't use or own a razor. In fact, I didn't shave the soft hairs off my legs because I refused to hold a razor in my hands.

But now my fingers shook, calling to me like an angel of mercy, begging me to take that next step.

Do it, Rowan. Do it. You know you want to. You'll feel better.

But where? My other arm? My thighs that were always covered by shorts or jeans? My stomach?

Mike's razor was down the hall. I left it in the medicine cabinet in the bathroom on purpose, a sort of courage check—would I use it? Would I not?

From the sounds coming up the stairs, voices and music mixed with Delilah's barking, the house was already filling with people. The razor called to me, though. Its siren song wove through the air like a tide rushing in, rushing toward me.

My chest rose with each fast, shallow breath. Mike's razor was like a tiny security blanket, ready and waiting. When I first moved in, knowing the razor was there had been a daily test to see if I could make it through the day without wrenching it out of its hard, plastic case.

And I had made it, day by day. But right now, each limb shook with anticipation. The decision was made. The release was near. I couldn't wait. There would be help for me now. I'd make it through this night, through Mike's leaving tomorrow. Through Dad's return. Through everything else that was spinning out of control.

I may have even laughed out loud. I wasn't sure.

I reached for my robe, counting the number of seconds it would take me to dash to the bathroom and dart back. I would lock the door, throw the robe across the floor onto the piles of shoes, and finally feel like I had some sort of control in my life.

Just as my fingers brushed against the soft cotton, someone knocked on the door.

"ROWAN? IT'S me." My lungs deflated and my shoulders fell. Jess' knock and words woke me from my trance. "Rowan, open up."

I was still wearing only the boots and my underwear so I threw on my robe and yanked opened the door. Jess breezed in, her oil-slicked hair falling down around her face, the blonde roots a runway down her scalp.

"Why aren't you dressed?" She shoved the shoes off the bed and lay down on top of the pile of clothes.

"I'm working on it." I clenched and unclenched my fingers, still yearning for the coolness of the steel.

"You okay?" Jess' blue eyes narrowed, her thick glasses falling down her nose.

I slumped to the floor. Defeated. Deflated. I had come so far. How could I go back there? To cutting? To lying? To covering up? If I didn't stop, I'd carve up my entire body before I hit twenty.

I studied Jess as she looked at me. Jess was my best friend. She never judged me. Ever. But I couldn't talk to her about this. Not yet. Maybe never.

"Yeah. I'm fine. It's just been a long couple of days."

"Uh-huh. I'm sure."

I picked at my cuticle and pulled a hanging piece of skin from the side of my nail. A bubble of blood appeared, and I smeared it with my thumb. "Yeah. I mean, I guess. When does Paul get back?"

She shrugged and started picking at her own cuticles. "I haven't heard from him."

"You haven't heard from Paul? Is he okay?"

She shrugged and started chewing the side of her nail. "I haven't heard from him," she repeated. "It's weird, ya know?" She flipped onto her back and stared at the ceiling.

"What's weird?" I got up and rummaged through the clothes, making an effort to keep my voice steady and normal.

"I don't know. Everything, I guess."

"Being pregnant?" I asked, trying to lure the thoughts out of her head so they could replace my own.

"Yeah. I guess. I mean…I don't know." She flipped back to her stomach and yanked her glasses off. She rubbed her eyes until she peered at me from red, swollen lids. "So get dressed already. Or don't you want to go downstairs? We could hang up here all night. I don't mind if we miss the par-tay. We could sneak out and go get something to eat. I'm starving."

"Nah." I grabbed a pair of my old, pre-Anderson jeans and my old blue hoodie. "We'll go. He's leaving tomorrow. If I don't see him tonight then what? Summer? Spring soccer season will start soon and then there's no hope of a visit with all the games they play."

"Are you going to school tomorrow?"

"Of course. Aren't you?"

She shrugged. Jess didn't share my sentiment that college was the meal ticket out of here. "Yeah. Sure." She spit a fingernail onto the floor.

"Gross."

She laughed. "I know."

The tingling was gone from my fingers. I exhaled, the whoosh of breath mixing with the distant sound of voices downstairs. Jess burst out laughing again.

"What?" I demanded, putting my hands on my hips, ignoring the sharp points of my bones.

"You look like a freak show."

I glanced down at my scuffed black boots and my short white robe. I started to giggle, low at first, until I burst out laughing. Soon we were laughing so hard I fell onto the bed beside her, gasping for breath.

"What's going on in there?" Mike pounded on the door, making us laugh even harder.

"I hope you're decent because I'm coming in."

I was laughing so hard I couldn't protest. Mike threw open the door and stood in the doorway, dressed in pressed khakis and a navy blue polo shirt. His mouth fell open when he saw us on the bed, clutching each other, tears running down our faces.

"What on earth is wrong with the two of you?" But he started laughing, too. He held out a hand to each of us and we sat up, wiping our faces.

"You two are crazy. Everyone's here. Are you guys coming down or are you planning to stay up here all night? Rowan, you might want to put on some clothes."

My robe had fallen open at the waist. I scrambled to fix it before it exposed anything I didn't want it to.

"I'll be right there. I just have to change." I wiped my eyes with the back of my hand.

"Okay." He walked to the door then turned back to us. "I like the boots, Rowan. You should wear them tonight. They're more... *you.*"

He closed the door with a *click*.

chapter six

"YOU SURE you want to go down there?" She wove her arm through mine. "We could just walk out the front door."

"I wish." *Thud. Thud. Thud* went our boots as we walked down the stairs. "But Mike is leaving tomorrow. If I don't see him tonight, I don't know when I'll see him again."

"Good point, I guess. Why don't you skip school and go to his game?"

We stopped at the bottom stair, the voices of a house full of people filling the air. Why couldn't I miss a few days of school? I hadn't missed any this year. My grades were good. I was either going to get into the colleges to which I applied or I wasn't. The next three days wouldn't make a difference.

"No. I can't."

"Why not? It's not like it matters now." Jess bent down several inches to look me in the eye.

Instead of meeting her gaze, I scanned the living room. Three church ladies sat side by side on the sofa, clutching teacups and staring at the opposite wall. They didn't turn at the sound of our voices.

"Ro?" Jess yanked on my arm. "Why don't you just go?"

The thought left a bad taste in my mouth, like I had just swallowed a sour piece of apple. "No. I need to go to school."

"Oh yeah? Why?"

If a gaze could burn through layers of skin, Jess' would have. When laughter erupted from the kitchen, I pulled her forward. "Let's go." I didn't hear Mike's familiar laugh within that outburst, but he was down here somewhere and my stomach did flips thinking about seeing him.

When we walked into the kitchen, I found who I was looking for. Mike was standing by the counter talking to his dad and his high school soccer coach. He was leaning against the granite with his feet crossed at the ankle, his broad shoulders relaxed, arms sluggishly crossed over his hard stomach. Without realizing it, I pulled my lip between my teeth to keep myself from letting out a squeal. Seeing him back in this house was just about the best sight I could imagine.

He glanced up when Jess and I walked in. A grin pulled his lips wide. He threw a hand up and waved. The smile disappeared as swiftly as it appeared, and he turned back to his dad and coach.

I stayed there, rooted in the doorway, waiting on him to tell his dad and coach that he'd talk to them later; waiting on him to come to me. Instead, they walked outside without a backward glance.

"Why didn't he come over here?" Jess demanded.

"He's been anxious to see his coach." There was no point mentioning they'd spent the morning together.

Mrs. Anderson was laughing at the other end of the counter with a couple of Mike's friends. I knew almost everyone there. Most were his old soccer teammates and their girlfriends who'd I'd gotten to know over the summer. I waved to a few who called out my name.

His friend, Jonathan, popped out of his seat and strolled over. "Hey girls." He leaned a shoulder against the wall and smiled at Jess.

"Hi, Jon," I said, to mask the silent treatment Jess was giving him. She had less than zero interest in high school boys.

"Hey, Ro." Jon kept his gaze on Jess but steered his words in my direction. "So, bummer that he has to leave so soon, but I'm sure the two of you have a blast when you go up to visit. Having his own place and all." His thick brown brows were raised high, and he still hadn't looked at me.

Jess folded her arms and huffed.

"Um, yeah. It's great," I said.

"You do get to go up, right? You know for a little quiet time?" When Jonathan said *quiet time* he leaned down and dropped his voice to a whisper, his dark eyes flashing with all the perverted thoughts that were rolling through his head. He let out a soft chuckle that grated against my nerves and made me want to put on more clothes.

What I didn't tell him was that I had only visited Mike once and that was on a trip with his parents so I stayed in the hotel room with them. There was no *quiet time* that weekend. I also didn't tell him that Mike hadn't gone to great lengths to invite me up for a visit.

True I was busy—I had work, school, etc. But Mike was always busy with games, studying, parties. Only once had he mentioned me coming up for a party that his fraternity was throwing. Except it was a weekend when Janie was out of town, and I had to work.

"Jon!" Someone from the other side of the room called his name.

He pushed off the wall and stood. "Well, ladies, it was nice chatting with you. Rowan, good to see you again." For the first time since he came to pay us a visit, Jon pulled his eyes from Jess and looked down at me. It only lasted a second. "Jess, call me sometime." He winked, seemingly oblivious that Jess hadn't said one word to him.

"High school guys are so creepy." Jess snarled her lip. "I much prefer an older man."

Mike was still outside with his dad and coach, only now he had been joined by two girls I didn't know. They weren't from school—ours wasn't so large that I didn't at least recognize everyone, even if I didn't know their names. These girls were tall with long blonde hair that fell down their backs. Even from this distance, I could see heavy eye makeup, tight jeans jutting out from under their designer coats, and long, slim legs filling the denim in a way my skinny ones never did.

Suddenly, one of the girls burst into laughter so loud, I could hear it all the way in the kitchen. She doubled over and as giggles trailed the outburst like little bells, she put a hand on Mike's arm.

"I think I'm ready to go," I managed.

"I think that's a good idea," Jess agreed.

Just as I grabbed her elbow to dart back upstairs, someone came up behind me and threw their arms around my neck, nearly choking me. "Hey, Sis!" Trina planted a wet kiss on my cheek, making me cringe and my insides scream.

I wrenched myself free. "Trina, what are you doing here?"

Trina lifted a shoulder then dropped it—the *whatever* move she'd perfected over the years. "I came with Jennifer. She's dating Brandon now." Brandon was on the high school soccer team and had played with Mike last year.

Trina popped her gum, and I was hit with a blast of minty breath. "So what? You know this party kinda sucks. A little lame with the old ladies. I mean, who invited them? Seriously, geriatric town in the house!" Her words burst out of her mouth in rapid-fire. "I mean, seriously. And only soda to drink? Is he in college or what? Couldn't he provide something a little," she leaned toward us, "stronger?" She popped the gum, and her eyes darted around the room.

Trina had on skintight black jeans that barely covered her butt and a loose-fitting top that fell off the shoulder, showing a purple bra strap underneath. Blonde hair fell down her back in a golden sheet. Her lipstick was pink and her eye makeup was heavy and slightly smudged. The smell of pungent perfume quickly replaced the smell of her gum. But it was her large pupils and fast talk that left my brows pursed.

"What are you on, Trina?"

"Huh?" Her head was whipping around the room, turning from one corner to the next and back again.

"Trina, are you high?"

She shrugged and screamed the name of her friend. "Jennifer! I'm over here."

Her friend, the only one I think she had, waved and winked from the corner of the room where she huddled with Brandon, her hand rubbing a path over his chest. He had his hand on the back of her jeans, one finger hooked through her belt loop. She flashed Trina a thumbs-up and Trina turned back to me. "You're too skinny, Ro. You look like a skeleton again."

"Go to hell," Jess seethed.

Trina glared at Jess, but her expression was back to peaches and cream and bright eyes when she turned to me. "Why don't you come by the house tomorrow after school? Dad is dying to see you. Gran can make dinner. You know. Just like old times when she used to come over and you know, pick up the slack from Mom. Chicken and dumplings, spaghetti, steak. I don't know. I mean, whatever you want. She misses you *terribly*." Her voice oozed with fake drama. She started to bounce up and down on her feet.

When Hell freezes over was on the tip of my tongue, but I didn't say it. Whatever she was on, there was no point talking to her. "Sorry, Trina. Can't." I turned, but she grabbed my arm and yanked me to a stop.

"Ro." As if on cue, her blue eyes filled with tears. "I just want us to be friends. Can't we just be friends? Sisters again?"

I slid away from her, my skin burning from her touch.

"Go away you little tramp," Jess spat. "Crawl back to your dealer for a little pick-me-up. You're going to crash soon."

Trina gasped then cried out. Mrs. Anderson was by my side in a second.

"Ladies, what's going on?" She looked between the three of us, her arm around my waist.

With a glare at my sister, I answered, "Nothing, Mrs. A. My sister was just leaving."

Trina pulled her lips into a wide smile, morphing her face until she looked like a porcelain angel. "Mrs. Anderson, I'm so sorry to bother you. I just needed to speak with my sister. And," her lips fell from the smile to a trembling, pursed line, "to apologize to you for last year. I'm...I'm so ashamed." Tears streamed down her heavily blushed cheeks.

Mrs. Anderson's mouth fell open. Trina clutched her stomach then doubled over, bursting into sobs. Mrs. Anderson's eyes widened. When Trina's wails filled the air, Mike's mom pulled her into a hug. Mike's friends were staring. Jon was smirking. Trina's friend, Jennifer, had a hand over her mouth, laughing. And I wanted to shrink into a hole.

Trina looked like she could barely stand up, the weight of her pain was so heavy. Mrs. Anderson led her to the kitchen table, scattering Mike's friends, and eased her into a chair. When Trina's sobs wracked through her body again, Mrs. Anderson pulled my sister to her, holding her tight, much the same way she'd held me my first night in this home.

Jess pulled at my arm, trying to get me to follow Mike's friends into the living room. But I was rooted to that spot. Horror ripped through me in talon-like shreds as I watched. It was unbelievable—Mrs. Anderson comforting my lying, deceitful, high-on-drugs sister.

I wanted to scream. Never had I witnessed a scene so ugly, so gut-wrenching, so vile. Mrs. Anderson and Trina? Mike seemed to agree. He was watching them through the window, a frown on his face.

JESS AND I left before the party was over and went to Mario's. Jess was starving again, and I had to get out of that house.

Just as a large pizza was set in front of us, I got a text from Mike.

Where are you?

At Mario's with Jess.

Want to meet? I want to see you.

Jess chomped on the crust of her first piece of pizza and grabbed another before she even swallowed.

> I'll be done in an hr. I'll pick you up in front of the house.

It didn't even take an hour for Jess to finish half the pizza. I had one slice, then we put the rest in a box and left. She was half asleep before we even pulled out of the parking lot, so I took her home then swung by the Anderson's to pick up Mike. He was waiting on the porch outside. The driveway was empty of his friends' cars and most of the house's lights were turned off.

"Hey." He climbed into the passenger seat.

"Hi." I leaned forward so he could kiss me. His mouth tasted like toothpaste. Minutes later, I asked, "Where should we go?"

"Usual spot."

I bit my lip with the promise of those words as I drove down the road toward Beauty Mountain.

Mike pushed his hand into my hair, warming the back of my neck. "I need some time with you."

Tingles shot up and down my skin. Finally. Finally we were going to have a minute. It wasn't much. He was still leaving in less than twelve hours. But it was something. And it was enough. It had to be.

The sky was clear, the moon and stars helping light the way. His thumb caressed the back of my neck. "What happened back there with Trina?"

My shoulders tightened. "I don't know. She just…showed up."

He looked out the side window. "I sure didn't expect to see her there." He sighed. "I don't care if I never see her again."

"I know. Your mom didn't seem to have those same feelings." I clenched my teeth, regretting the dig as soon as it came out. Mrs. Anderson had a big, kind heart. She would never turn someone away, no matter what they had done.

"I know. It was definitely a strange sight." His hand dropped from my neck.

We rode the rest of the way in silence. I knew he was lost in last year's events the same as I was. But I was determined not to dwell on the past. Not tonight. So I put my hand on his thigh and made sure his thoughts were on something else besides Trina.

chapter seven

"I HAVE something for you." Mike ran his fingers through my hair. We were parked at Beauty Mountain, the lookout just yards away. It was too cold to get out of the heated car and the snow had started to fall again. The only light came from the dashboard. The radio was on but turned so low I couldn't tell what song was playing.

"What is it?" Mike and I were facing each other in the front seat. My hand was on his thigh, my thumb tracing small circles over the top of his jeans, the events from the day all but forgotten.

"You better stop that or you'll have to wait for the present."

I laughed and moved my hand a little higher. He leaned toward me and it was several minutes before either of us spoke again. By then the moon was obscured through the foggy windows, and I pulled away with a giggle. "Um, did you say you have something for me?"

His eyes were dark in the dim light. "I almost forgot."

He laughed and so did I, suddenly shy and nervous. It was only months ago when he'd given me a delicate pair of tiny gold hoop earrings that I wore every day. When he pulled out another small velvet box, my heart caught in my throat.

"Here." He held his hand toward me. "It's just a little something. I'm sorry I haven't seen more of you. And that I'm leaving again so soon."

I hesitated until he pried open my fingers and laid the box in my palm. When I opened it, yellow gold caught the light from the dashboard. He pulled the box from me and took the ring out.

"Let's see if it fits." He took my hand in his and slipped the ring on my right ring finger. It slid back off.

"Shit," he said. "I even tried it on. I thought if it fit my pinky, it would fit."

"Try my middle finger."

He did. The ring fit that finger perfectly. It was a thick band with three woven strands, no stones, intricate and shiny.

"Mike, I don't know what to say." He held my hand up toward the dashboard. "It's beautiful." The ring was heavy and cool. I was unused to wearing rings and it felt foreign, but in a good way.

"I know it's hard with me being gone so much. It'll be easier when you come to the university next year."

I nodded, watching the red dots of light reflect off the gold. Mike assumed that I was going to the same university as him. And that was a good option. But there were other options, too. "It depends on where I get the most financial aid." It seemed a strange thing to say when he'd just given me a gift and seemed excited about us being together soon. Except he just assumed, despite how many times I stressed otherwise, that I would go to the same school as him. I guess when you grow up with all the money and opportunity you could dream of, you didn't worry about things like financial aid.

"Well, yeah, I know. But I'm sure you'll be there. I mean, it's the best school in the state."

"That small liberal arts college is actually really good. Miss J. is always talking about it." I bit my lip. I didn't want to be argumentative, especially now. But sometimes I couldn't help myself. As much as I loved being here with him tonight, alone and without distractions, the events of the day were picking at my nerves, making them feel raw and exposed.

He pulled my hand into his. "Yeah. That school is good enough. But the university is better. More fun. You'll love it."

There was no point saying that I didn't think I would love it as much as he thought I would. I wasn't a crowd-loving type of girl and the university was swarming with students, nearly thirty thousand. I also didn't say that my dad was back in town, that Trina was acting weird again, or that I felt more like an alien every day living in his home without him actually being there. So many things simply went unsaid.

Instead, I muttered, "I'm sure I would love it." I leaned in and kissed his neck. He didn't say another word about where I would go to college. Or anything else for that matter.

THAT NIGHT when Mike came into my room, I didn't bother to set the alarm on my phone. It was foolish. Irresponsible. Disrespectful. But knowing he was leaving early in the morning made me set my phone on the nightstand and intentionally not think of the consequences.

I slept in the crook of Mike's arm, snuggled into his neck. His scent filled my nose each time I inhaled. His chest rose and fell under the warmth of my hand. His leg was heavy as it laid over mine, but I didn't pull away, even when it made my foot go numb.

I stayed awake far after his gentle snores began, listening to his breathing, feeling his skin beneath my fingers, relishing the nearness of him. At one point I lifted my hand and held it up for the dim nightlight to catch the gold of the ring. It was so beautiful. I could have never imagined that someone would give me something so beautiful. But it also made me sad, almost like it was a consolation prize. I put my arm back under the covers.

He was leaving, and he'd helped me feel better by giving me jewelry. What he didn't know, or maybe he did, was that I would trade almost anything to be near him and not have him leave me again. But that hope was futile. Out in the hallway were his bags, packed and ready for a very early departure. He would leave before I even needed to get up for school. And his parents would leave with him. And I'd be all alone in a house that wasn't my home.

I could go, too. But for reasons I didn't completely understand, I wouldn't. When I clutched his arm, he moaned and pulled away. I laid awake for hours thinking.

Where did I belong?

Was there a place in this world for me?

The thought had me yanking up my shirtsleeve. I stared at the scars, the dozen angry slashes, and the *A* for Aidan that I'd carved into my arm.

One.

Two.

Three.

Four.

Five.

And on. And on. And on.

I forced myself to count each one. And with each number I forced myself to remember what it was like where I'd come from, and to appreciate where I was now. If I didn't fit in here with the Andersons, I didn't fit in back home either.

A picture of that run-down house popped into my head with its dry, brittle grass and broken shutters; my obese, unkempt mother. I saw my sister, with evil behind those blue eyes, accusing Mike of rape. Dad's fist. Gran's smile that hid the truth all those years.

And then I saw blood. Not dripping blood, but bubbles of blood—spots like those that peppered my skin after I cut. Blood droplets everywhere.

A cool chill like the embrace of a ghost washed over my skin. Scout's sweet purr was the only thing that held me tied to the present. I swallowed against the lump in my throat and scooped her up. Sadness was creeping toward me, threatening to surround me and consume me like poison. I had to keep it away. If I allowed it to enter, here in this house, even a slither of it, I would certainly be devoured. I wasn't sure if I was strong enough to deny it. I'd felt too many glimpses of it already.

Where did I belong?

I stroked Scout's head long into the night, struggling, and failing, to find an answer to that question.

SOMETIME TOWARD dawn, when the world was still cast in black, Mike turned over and wrapped his arms around me. I had finally fallen asleep and his touch felt like a dream. But it was a perfect dream and even as my mind remained foggy, my body was awake.

Later, I tumbled back to sleep, snuggled safely in Mike's arms with a smile spread across my face and his heat warming my heart.

Sunlight poured through the closed curtains, streaming in soft, white light, and I reached over. With eyes still closed, I tried to touch him, to ward off the morning for just a minute more.

When my hand found nothing but the cool pillowcase and empty space beside me, I sat up and listened for the sound of voices. The clock read six thirty and the house was like a concrete wall of silence—stifling, suffocating, frightening. Where was the noise? Mike and his parents should be bustling to get out the door. Had something changed?

I jumped out of bed and darted down the hall, stopping myself before I crashed into the window. If I'd jumped off a skyscraper, my heart wouldn't have plummeted more. There were no cars in the driveway except for my own. They'd left. Mike had left. His parents had left. He hadn't even said goodbye.

I fell to my knees, my chest hurting so bad I doubled over and let my forehead hit the carpet. If silence had a sound, it was louder than the whip-like crack of thunder, more jolting than the piercing blare of a siren, more devastating than the rumbling bellow of a catastrophic earthquake.

SOMETIME LATER I peeled myself off the floor and stumbled back to my room. I grabbed my phone.

Come stay with me. Andersons are out of town.

I didn't expect Jess to answer but at least my message would be waiting for her when she checked her phone. She would come and stay with me. All she wanted was to get away from her dad and his new girlfriend.

I crawled back into bed. It felt cold and foreign, all the warmth and love gone. I burrowed under as far as I could and lifted onto my elbows. With my small book light turned on, I flipped to a new page in my journal.

The path is hidden
Behind a smoky curtain
So thick with tears
And pain
I can't see.
Is it there?
Does it exist?
Or will I, little Rowan Slone, get lost in the mist?

I slammed the journal shut. No one would ever see these poems. They were so stupid. *Stupid.* I threw the pen across the room.

When my phone started to ring, I lunged for it so fast, I knocked it off the nightstand and had to crawl under the bed to get it. By the time I fished it out it had gone to voice mail. But I could see who called—my grandmother. The voicemail box lit up to tell me she'd left a message.

Hi, Rowan. It's Gran. Trina told me that you know your dad is back in town. Can you come over for dinner tonight? I think it would be good if you could see him. Being as stubborn as he is, he may not call you. But I know he wants to see you. He keeps asking if you're coming home. I don't think he believes me when I tell him that you haven't been here since last May.

She released a heavy sigh, her breath bristling through the phone. *I miss you. I wonder if you've spent any time with Trina. Something seems to be going on with her. I'm just not sure what. But I trust you'll tell me if there's anything I need to know.*

Please come to dinner tonight. I'll make chicken and dumplings. I hope they're still your favorite. If you can't come over, at least call me. Her voice cracked. *I love you, sweetheart.*

My gran had known that my mom was the one who killed Aidan. She'd known it the day after he died. And she'd kept the secret all that time.

Part of me could understand. How difficult would it be to turn your own child in for murder? And for me, I was only ten and she didn't think anything would come of it. His death was a natural cause. Putting the blanket on him was not a criminal offense.

But she couldn't know how devastating the past years had been. Aidan's death had shaped every single part of my life. It had formed my relationships with Mom, Dad, Trina, even myself. I failed the fifth grade because I couldn't cope. The guilt that had weighed down my thin shoulders was so much it was amazing I could hold myself up.

I deleted the message. Almost immediately there was a text. It was from Jess.

> Where are they?
>
> At Mike's game. I don't want to stay here alone.
>
> That's right. I forgot. Let me see if Paul is around tonight. I'll definitely come over tomorrow if not today.
>
> K.
>
> You ok?

But I flipped the phone closed. Beside my bed sat my earbuds. I shoved them into my ears and turned the volume all the way up on my iPod. Within a beat, the music was too loud for any thought to take hold—exactly what I wanted.

I lay there with my brain pulsing. Outside the window the sky was a dark gray, like it was so many winter days in this area. It wasn't snowing, though, and I was glad for Mrs. Anderson. She was always worried about the snow.

After an hour or so, I turned off the music, my ears still ringing long after I pulled the buds out. I crept out of bed and grabbed the pen I'd thrown. I pulled out my journal. I'd write in it for *me,* even if the poems were stupid.

> *Will winter be gone,*
> *Or will it always reside?*
> *Will the darkness flitter away,*
> *Or will it never subside?*

I stared out the window until the cap of the pen was chewed flat. I lifted Scout off the bed and went downstairs to check on the dogs. Levi bounded toward the door, pawing at the white wood. Delilah snorted at me from the couch but didn't move.

My phone dinged a new message, and I flipped it open.

Miss you already.

Just as I started to write *miss you too* something stopped me. Aggravation that he'd left again? Hurt that he hadn't said goodbye?

It wasn't right to hold his leaving against him. He didn't have a choice. Having been given a soccer scholarship, he had to do what the coaches wanted. But he didn't have to leave without waking me up and telling me goodbye.

The world beneath my feet was shaking, and I knew it would take everything I had to stay upright.

chapter eight

I STOOD at the window watching Levi try to get Delilah to wrestle in the backyard. It had been two hours since I had sent a text to Jess about coming over, and she couldn't get here fast enough. The silence in this large house was so heavy it was suffocating.

When the phone dinged again, I hurried to open it. It was from Jess.

> Be over in an hour. How long can I stay?

> Andersons back in two days. You can stay till then.

> Good. I need to get out of here before I do something I'll regret.

JESS SHOWED up sooner than I expected. Her eyes were red-rimmed, swollen, and glassy. It was hard to tell if she was just tired or had been crying. My instincts told me it was the latter but when I asked if everything was okay, she said it was and walked away.

Later that evening when we were making spaghetti for dinner, I asked her again. She'd been quiet and moody all day. Between the two of us, you'd think our lives were ending. I knew my friend and knew she was pregnant, but was there something more?

I was thawing frozen meatballs in marinara sauce while Jess stared out the window. A heavy snow had started to fall, but I didn't think it was the fluffy flakes that held her attention. Her shoulders were slumped and every now and then she wiped at her eyes.

"Okay, Jess. Spill it." I stood at the counter with a hand on my hip.

"Huh?" She wiped her eyes again and looked at me over her shoulder.

"Jess, what's going on?"

"It's nothing."

"Tell me. I'm not going to quit asking."

She didn't face me as she wrapped her arms around her stomach. "Paul's gone."

I dumped the pasta into the colander. "Gone? Back to Colorado? I thought he just got home."

I pulled two plates out of the cabinet and placed them on the table, stopping near her side.

"He never came back."

My hands stopped midair. "What do you mean *he never came back*?"

Jess walked toward the counter and stirred the marinara sauce. "When he went to Colorado he never came back."

"Well…have you heard from him? Is everything okay?" Was he dead in a ditch somewhere?

Several seconds passed and I walked around the counter, moving toward her on heavy feet. I placed my hand on her shoulder. She stopped stirring.

"He's not coming back. He is staying in Colorado. Without me."

Levi padded into the room. He licked Jess' hand, and her fingers brushed over his fur. Finally she turned to me, tears filling her blue eyes.

"It's over. He's not coming back, and I'm not going out to be with him." She yanked off her glasses and wiped at her eyes.

"What happened?"

She inhaled a shaky breath. "He's just done. He doesn't want me...us."

"Does he know you're pregnant?" My voice was hushed like I didn't want to give away a secret.

She slumped over the counter, her head in her hands.

My hand rubbed her back sympathetically. The question lingered in the air like a menacing buzz.

"He knows," she sobbed.

"He knows you're pregnant and he's not coming back? Jess, that doesn't make any sense. Maybe he's going to find a job?" My head tilted to the side—like that would help rebalance my brain.

Her tears fell onto the counter in tiny droplets. "He told me that he wasn't ready to be a father. That I should *take care of it*, and he didn't mean take care of a baby."

"He wants you to have an abortion?"

She nodded, running her hands through her greasy hair. "That's his answer." She stood and wiped her nose with the back of her hand. "He said that he wanted to break things off for a while. That he had been planning to go to Colorado alone for weeks; he just wasn't sure how to tell me. So when I told him I was pregnant—*poof*—he's off to Colorado for good."

Nausea and fury erupted in waves, tearing through my stomach. My fingers shook with rage. *How dare he?*

But I had to bite my tongue. She seemed so sad, like a little girl lost in a meadow of tall grass where she couldn't see a way out, where there was no way out.

I pulled out a kitchen chair and lightly pushed her toward it until she sat down. I gently grasped her hands in mine, and we talked long into the night.

MY ALARM went off early the next morning, but Jess and I were still awake. We had never gone to sleep. We were lying on my bed still talking—about Mike, Paul, pregnancy, parents, what she was going to do.

"Guess we'd better get ready." I rolled over and scooped Scout into my arms. She lay on my chest, warm and purring, her wet nose nudging my chin any time I stopped petting her.

"Are you awake?" I expected Jess to start moaning—we'd just been talking not five minutes ago. But her breath had deepened. I leaned over her. The circles under her eyes had grown darker over the past weeks like little black half-moons against a pale sky.

I laid Scout down beside her and went to take a quick shower. When I went back to my bedroom she was snoring softly. Scout was curled into a small, furry ball on the pillow by her head. I didn't know if I should wake her or not so as I got ready, I made more noise than I needed to, keeping an eye on her. She didn't budge, though, even when I accidentally knocked a box of shoes off a shelf in the closet.

It felt so good to wear my old boots the other day that I rummaged through my things until I found an old pair of jeans. When I moved in with the Andersons, I'd put on weight and these jeans had become too tight—the first time I'd *ever* put on clothes that were too tight. Now they fit like a well-worn glove. Guess those eight pounds were gone.

I found my hoodie and pushed my feet into my old boots. I put in the earrings Mike gave me and slid the ring on my finger. Except it didn't feel right. It felt too heavy and awkward against my skin even though it was a perfect fit. I put it back in its box and went to wake Jess.

"Time to get up." I pushed her shoulder. "Jess? Get up." Still no answer. "Jess!"

"Huh?" Her voice was muffled in the pillow.

"It's time for school. You know that place you go to learn."

"I'm not going. Too tired." Scout pawed at Jess' hair.

"Come on, Jess. You can't miss the first day back."

"I can do whatever I want. I'm eighteen."

"You're not eighteen."

"Close enough."

"I'll make breakfast. Go shower, and I'll get something ready."

"Okay. But then I'm coming back to bed." She flipped to her side, putting her back to me.

I sighed as she yanked the covers over her head.

"Fine." I left the room. I didn't make her breakfast. She could fend for herself when she got up. I let Levi outside and was hit with a blast of freezing air.

"Come on, Delilah. Go outside. I have to leave."

The bulldog barely cracked open one eye before promptly shutting it again.

"Fine. Jess can let you out."

I grabbed my empty backpack and pulled on the winter coat Tabitha had given me. It was a designer coat—one of those that had the label on the chest, the same coat all the popular girls wore to school. It really wasn't my style, but it did keep me warm. I found my keys and left through the front door, locking it behind me.

TWO BLOCKS away I realized I didn't have gas, and I pulled into the nearest station. I had remembered my phone today and checked it one more time to see if Jess had changed her mind but the screen was blank.

After putting the nozzle in the car, I went into the food mart to get a coffee. I walked out the door and was halfway through my first sip when I jolted to a stop in the middle of the parking lot, spilling coffee down the front of my jacket. My car sat before me, the gas line snaking out of the side like a black, ominous reptile. But it was the person standing beside it that sent tremors through my blood like an earthquake.

A car beeped at me to move and I stepped forward, coffee forgotten, legs numb, head scrambling to read the mood of the man standing just inches from my car. My dad was back, staring straight at me with eyes that didn't blink. I was only safe if I could read his moods. *And I couldn't read his mood.*

I stopped at the front of my car. He stood toward the back on the other side of the hose. It wasn't a great barrier but it was something. Counting didn't calm me as the only memory that kept popping up in my head was the image of his fist barreling toward my face.

His posture was more stooped than I remembered. His back had a curve that I could see even facing him head-on. He had lost weight, making his clothes hang on his body like a scarecrow that had lost its stuffing.

His eyes stared at me from beneath the shadow of a worn-out hat. He didn't blink. He looked exhausted; his eyes resembled giant, glassy marbles that were sunk deep within his pasty skin.

His lips were pulled into a thin, pale line. I had become a master at reading my dad's facial expressions, but I couldn't read the one on his face now and that, more than his abrupt appearance, scared me.

"What are you doing here?" I swallowed against the shaking in my voice.

He took one step forward, his knee pushing against the hose. "Rowan." There was no greeting in his words or an expression on his face. One hand hung by his side; the other shoved in the pocket of his old coat.

I cleared my throat. "What are you doing here?" I repeated.

He raised his hand, palm facing me, and held it midair. He pulled in a loud breath. His hand was shaking. A slight tremor shot through it every few seconds making it jerk. "I came to check on you and Trina."

My heart started racing. "Why?" The word escaped my mouth like a burst of gunfire.

He took another step forward. My eyes never left him, flipping between the way he held his face and the way he held his hands. As soon as those fingers curled into themselves, forming a fist, I would run.

Anger, resentment, and barely veiled hatred had always simmered through him like a disease. I didn't have a single memory from my childhood when he smiled or was happy. His dad had forced him to marry my mom, and he had resented all of us ever since. When Aidan was born, he brought light into our lives and gave us all a tiny morsel of hope.

My dad was finally trying to be present, part of the family, content. He had his son and we all thought that maybe things would change. And they did…for a while. But then I put that blanket on Aidan. Within the paintbrush stroke of one night, everything in our lives changed, imploded, and fell apart.

The man standing before me, though, was almost unrecognizable because I couldn't find the anger and resentment that I'd grown so familiar with. It wasn't in his expression, his posture, the look behind his eyes. It wasn't in the rigid, straight back and proud shoulders. This was unchartered territory and it made me so uneasy I would've felt safer in the middle of the ocean with a swarm of hungry sharks closing in.

He ran a hand over his face. He'd aged since I'd last seen him. The wrinkles around his eyes and mouth were deeper. The scruff of his beard showed more white than dark brown. My dad had always been a tall man using his stature to intimidate, control. Right now, though, he looked like someone had pricked him with a needle, deflating the air, the life, out of him.

"I needed some time away." He rubbed his face again.

"You mean after you beat me up?" I regretted the verbal slap as soon as it left my mouth.

His lips thinned and his eyes hardened, dark shadows passing over his face.

I stepped back. *Run if you need to. Just run.*

Instead, he merely nodded.

Cars came and went while we stood there, only a few feet from each other. There was something about him—something darker, blacker, not sinister like I remembered but *infected*.

"Where did you go?" It didn't take much effort to sound distant, uncaring. He'd never cared about me. It had been pretty easy to quit caring about him—at least I told myself that.

"Here and there. I stayed with a friend in Baltimore—a guy I was in the service with. I needed to get my head on straight."

"Is your head on straight now?" Spikes and sharp knives flew in the air between us. I clenched my teeth as every cell in my body erupted in a frenzy. *What did he want?*

He stared at me, unblinking, for several moments. "I'll only say this one time, and you can take it or leave it."

I pulled in a breath and held it.

"I'm sorry…for what I did. And for not being a better father. It's just not me. Not in me. And you and Trina deserved better." He waved his hand through the air and shrugged as if he'd just made a comment about the weather and not about our lives.

chapter nine

IF HE had sprouted wings, grew a pig nose, and started flying I would've been less surprised. He was sorry? *Jack Slone was sorry?* I laid my hand on the hood of the car. It was still warm.

He shrugged again, as if to say, *That's it. That's all I have.* There was no emotion behind those haunted eyes of his; eyes that had followed me around the last several years of my life, always accusing, always watching.

Somewhere deep inside my brain words formed like seedlings. But they weren't taking root, and I found myself just staring.

"One more thing."

My mouth was still incapable of speech.

"I was at the VA the other day. Turns out I have lung cancer."

His demeanor was as casual as if he had just told me he had his teeth cleaned.

"You have cancer?" I choked. My brain tried to unravel and rewire with this information, shattering my long-held view of the most unreachable, cold man in the world. It seemed he was just that way to everything but cancer.

"Um, what do the doctors say? What treatment options are there? How…how long?"

"Six months. Maybe."

I stared hard at his face but couldn't detect a single flash of emotion anywhere. But I could see, and maybe I imagined it, where the cancer was eating away at him, hollowing out his cheeks, making the bones prominent and sharp; sinking in his eyes until he looked almost skeletal with one foot already in the ground.

"Six months?" I repeated.

"Maybe."

"Have you seen Mom?"

"No. But I know she's in jail." He didn't blink, his eyes round saucers. "I know the truth about what happened to the boy. It's all water under the bridge now, I guess. You've moved on from what Trina and your grandma say."

I almost burst out laughing. I've moved on? Was he serious? The sound caught in my chest, tugging at my heart.

"I'll be in town for a couple of weeks, I guess. Maybe we can catch up again. You're staying at the Anderson's?"

I nodded, suddenly so overcome with an urge to see him again, I said, "I still have the same cell number. Call me. Maybe we can go to dinner. Or something."

He gave one quick flip of his head and turned. He started to walk away.

"Do you need a ride?" I was surprised when the words came out of my mouth. I was even more surprised that I didn't want to see him go.

"No."

And he was gone, disappearing into the distance as I stood there. My coffee was cold, the hood of my car was cold, and yet inside, my heart felt the first crack of thawing toward my father.

THE DRIVE to school passed in a daze. My phone rang a couple of times—once from Mike and once from Gran. But I didn't answer it. What was there to say? After all this time, my dad shows up and tells me not only is he sorry for treating me like shit for most of my life, but hey, he also has cancer. I couldn't imagine carrying on a normal conversation right now.

Images of Jack Slone's life as I knew it flashed before me. Jack Slone in the high school yearbook pictures Mom used to show me. Jack Slone in a rage each time he and Mom got into a fight. Jack Slone's expression when he realized his son was dead. Jack Slone's fist coming toward my face.

Once I hit Main Street I pulled over, sobbing into the steering wheel. He was dying? How could I hate a man who was dying? How could I *not* hate a man who hated me? Had hated me all my life?

Tears poured down my cheeks in a torrent. Once I allowed one tear to escape it was over, and I lost control.

Aidan.

Dad.

Mom.

Trina.

Gran.

Rowan.

How did we all fit together in this miserable puzzle? Were we God's cruel joke? I could just see him up in Heaven laughing with Paul, or Peter, or whoever Mrs. Anderson's preacher said was up there with him.

We're bored. Let's destroy Rowan Slone's life.

How else could someone explain my life and what had happened to me?

Hiccups came and went before I flopped back against the seat. With the back of my hand I wiped away the moisture only to find the tears wouldn't stop.

I had just gotten used to the fact that my mother was a murderer. Now I had to get used to the fact that my dad was not only apologizing for everything he'd ever done, but was also dying?

I needed Mike. I needed to talk to him, to have him soothe the hurt. But he was five hours away at another soccer tournament, and I had no idea when I'd see him again.

"Oh God," I cried. "Oh God!" I buried my face in my hands, and the sobs wracked through my body with such fury I thought my ribs would break.

In the distance I could hear my phone ringing. It slowly eased me out of my stupor. I ignored it until it rang two more times. It was Miss J., my guidance counselor.

"Hello?" I croaked into the phone.

"Rowan, where are you? School started thirty minutes ago. Are you okay?"

I glanced at the clock. *Shit.* My college applications, including attendance and grades, were already out, but I still held onto the fear of slipping and never finding my feet again. School was the one thing that helped keep me on my feet.

"I'm coming. Sorry. I'll be there in ten minutes."

"What's wrong?" Miss J. knew me too well.

"Nothing. Everything. I'll get to school and come see you."

"Okay. See you in a few."

I flipped the phone shut, feeling such heaviness in my heart that I knew for sure it would stop working. I'd end up in a freshly dug grave right beside my dead father. And then my mom would eat herself to death, and she would be on the other side of Dad. It wouldn't be too long after that until Trina tried to kill herself again, or overdosed on whatever drugs she was taking. And she could be on the other side of Mom.

The Slone family plot at the cemetery. Is that how we'd all come back together? We'd all die and lose our lives of loneliness and despair only to end up back together for eternity? The thought sent a shuddering chill over my skin, like someone had just thrown me into a bath full of ice.

THE HALLS were quiet when I walked into the school. Everyone would be in second period by now. I should be in calculus, a class I really shouldn't miss. But instead of heading toward Room 23, I went to see my guidance counselor, Tanya Johnson.

There was a window cut into her wooden office door and I stood outside it, peering in. She was bent over her desk, dark brown hair falling around her face as she read the newspaper. One hand picked at a corner of the paper, while the other slapped lightly on a stack of papers on top of the messy desk, as if she were keeping a beat to music I couldn't hear.

I threw open the door and fell into the chair. My backpack hit the tiled floor with a loud *thud*.

Miss J. glanced up. A smile broke out over her face, making her large brown eyes appear as if they were also smiling, and then it swiftly disappeared. "Rowan, hello to you, too. How nice of you to show up." She shut the paper. "Now. What's going on?"

There was a loose thread on my jacket that I pulled until it came out. Then I twisted it around my finger, over and over until the tip turned white.

"Rowan!"

A soft sigh escaped my lips. "You know, it's been a tough year, right?"

"Yes… It's been quite a year, although are you referring to the actual past year or this school year? You need to be specific."

"I dunno. I mean, I guess the school year. But I can't ignore last year. Or the past eight years, can I? As much as I try, it never quite goes away."

"Why these somber thoughts? Do I need to ask again what's wrong?"

"I saw my dad." I twisted the thread.

"Your dad?" She leaned forward. "*Where?*" Her voice hardened.

"At the gas station this morning. I knew he was back." I waved a hand in the air and rolled my eyes. *This didn't bother me...this didn't bother me.* "Trina had told me he was back, but you know, who knew he'd come and find me."

"What did he want?"

"To tell me he's sorry."

"For...? What is he sorry for?"

"Who knows? Not loving me? Beating me to a pulp? Who can say?"

"Okay. Well, what else did he say?"

"He's dying."

"Your father's dying?"

"Seems as if."

"Rowan...Talk. Tell me what happened."

But I had already grown tired of this topic, probably because I still wasn't sure what to think about it.

Tanya Johnson had been my guidance counselor since my freshman year. Since I failed the fifth grade, the same year Aidan died, I'd had guidance counselors following my every move. Miss J. was the first one I actually liked talking to. That didn't mean I always opened up, but she made more headway than most when it came to talking about my life.

Silence filled the air now as she watched me play with the string. This office had become more familiar to me than my own locker. Could it be that it was only months ago that I sat in this chair, my face covered in heavy makeup just like my sister wore to mask the bruises that my father gave me?

I pushed to my feet and walked to the bookshelf. I let the thread fall to the floor then started straightening the brochures that lay there.

"Any word from the schools?" I asked her, my back turned.

"No. It's still too early. Don't worry. I'll let you know as soon as I get them."

When I sent in my college applications, I'd given them Miss J.'s mailing address. Sending them to my old home wasn't an option. They could have been sent to the Anderson's, but what if I had to leave for some reason? Or, well…it just seemed like the right thing to do.

The bell rang and I jumped. Miss J. chuckled and ran her fingers through her hair.

"Guess I need to go. I don't want to screw things up at this point in the game."

She came around her desk and stood by my side. "Rowan, you're doing just fine." She put her hand lightly on my shoulder, just a graze across the fabric of my coat.

I turned when I felt my eyes mist, hating and loving these pep talks. "See ya later."

"Okay. Have a good day."

After I passed through the door, I looked back at her. "You may not remember, but last year you told me that you were a testament that if you wanted something bad enough, you couldn't let anything stand in your way. What were you talking about?"

Her eyes clouded over, not with tears, but with memories come to life.

"Someday. But not today."

I nodded. Just before I walked out the door, I said, "By the way, I like your new haircut."

She touched the ends of her hair, newly cut into a style that fell to her shoulders. "Thanks, Rowan. That's sweet."

"Hot date? Is that why you cut it?"

"Out, Rowan." But she laughed, and so did I.

IT WAS lunchtime before I received a text from Jess.

> Have doc appt today. Can you come?
> What time?

5:00.

I'll be there.

The rest of the day passed in a blur of textbooks, notebooks, and furious note-taking. Miss. J. had told me to relax at the end of last quarter; that I was either in college or I wasn't; that I had a scholarship or I didn't. She said to ease up and then laughed at her advice since she *was* my guidance counselor.

Her suggestion made sense but the last thing I wanted to do was get into college with a scholarship and then lose it because I didn't understand the class content. Each time I thought of this, I buried my head deeper and deeper into the books.

My backpack weighed ten tons when I left the building. So much for lightening the load on seniors. Jess shouldn't miss too many more days. I had gone around and picked up the work she'd missed, but I could only do that for so long.

My phone dinged. It was Mike.

Can you talk?

I slid the phone into my pocket. There was so much to talk to him about that I wasn't sure I could talk about anything. *Oh well. Now is not a good time for me.* Maybe I'd call him after Jess' appointment.

It took awhile for my car to warm. Rubbing my hands together, I glanced around. The parking lot was already half empty. There were some students standing by the entrance to the school trying to sneak a cigarette.

In a car a few spaces over, I saw Trina, her blonde hair pulled into a messy ponytail high on top of her head. She was turned toward a guy in the driver's seat and didn't see me. There was only one car between us, and I had a clear view through that car's windows.

The guy was doing something with his hands in the space between them, though I couldn't tell what. But then Trina bent down, stayed there several seconds, sat up, and fell back against the seat. Now I could see the side of her face. Her eyes were closed.

Her lips were lifted into a smile. I'd never seen her look so calm and peaceful.

The guy leaned over and started to kiss her neck. As if sensing me near, her lids slowly opened, and her head turned toward the window. When she saw me, her smile faded and her eyes hardened. She lifted her hand, wiped the very tip of her nose, and pulled a long drag off a joint as the guy shoved his hand down her shirt.

I frowned all the way back to the Anderson's.

chapter ten

AS WE drove the twenty minutes to the free clinic Jess was quiet in the seat beside me, her black hair washed and frizzy. She had on an old white sweatshirt with a hole in the sleeve and a pair of jeans that I'd only seen her wear once before—when she had the stomach flu and I'd brought her chicken soup. Jess didn't do jeans but I guess today was different.

A light, freezing rain pattered across the windshield. Even the bare trees seemed to buckle from the weight of the thick sky. It matched my mood perfectly and something told me it matched hers, too.

"Are you okay?" When she didn't respond, I raised my voice. "Jess? Are you okay?"

Her chest rose and fell. She turned to me, her face lit brighter than a light bulb, almost as if she'd flipped a switch and her game face was on. "I'm great. Never better. I was just thinking of names."

I glanced at her again from the corner of my eye then turned my focus to the logging trucks taking up both lanes in front of me.

Neither of us said anything the rest of the drive and soon we were at the clinic. The entrance was down a few steps leading into the basement of a square, brick building, darkened by years of dirt and pollution. Two dead plants sat on either side of the doorway as a rather somber welcoming.

"Great place." Jess threw open the door, nearly hitting me in the head. "Very charming."

I rolled my eyes and followed her inside the windowless room. The air was stagnant and stale making me sneeze. Sickness hung in the air, along with the overpowering smell of antiseptic. It threatened to suffocate me, and I fell into the seat closest to the door while Jess went to check in.

Soon she was in the seat beside me, popping her bubble gum, and staring down at a clipboard.

"Do you want to come in with me?"

"If you want me to, I will. But aren't you going to, like, have to get undressed for this exam? Do you really want me in there?"

She blew a big bubble and let it pop. "Good point. That's okay. I thought I'd just have to pee on another stick, but I might get more than I bargained for." She bent over the clipboard, running her pen down the numbers. "I don't know any of this stuff. It's ridiculous. I shouldn't have to fill this out just so they can tell me my life is over."

"It's not over. Don't be a drama queen." If she noticed the lack of conviction in my voice she didn't say anything.

"My God, what is wrong with those people?" Jess cringed as she stared across the room.

A family took up the row across from us—what looked like a father, mother, and their three snotty, dirty children. The youngest kid cried nonstop, a croupy, congested awful sound that made me want to bathe in sanitizer.

Jess picked at her cuticle and tiny chips of black nail polish fell onto the paper.

"Jess." I touched her arm. "It'll be okay."

She watched the crying child and nodded, though something told me she didn't agree with my statement. Instead of filling out the paperwork, she started pulling out single strands of hair and letting it mix in with the black chips of polish.

"Jessica? Is there a Jessica here? There's no last name given." A thin, pasty-skinned woman stood in the doorway that led to the back. She wore faded pink scrubs and fanned her face with a yellow folder, looking as bored as I'd ever seen anyone look.

"You didn't give them your last name?" I asked Jess.

She jumped up, clipboard firmly in hand, the papers as empty of her information as they were when she sat down. "Nope. This is a covert operation."

"Jessica...?" the nurse called again.

I tugged at her sleeve. "You'd better go."

Suddenly that smile was back on her face. "Here!" She clomped across the room on heavy feet and bowed deeply to the bored nurse. "*Jessica* at your service." She sailed through the door and disappeared down the corridor.

One kid launched into an excruciatingly long cough that grated on my nerves worse than water torture. I pulled out homework, hoping for a distraction, but the kid's brother started crying. The mother darted toward the counter for a tissue, but by the time she got back the kid was crying so hard that snot ran all over his face and into his mouth. I ran outside, pulling in several gulps of the fresher air.

I found a spot that wasn't too dirty and sat on the curb. The wetness soaked through my jeans, although a wet butt was better than listening to the sick kids inside. The rain had stopped, but it was still cold and my fingertips numbed.

My homework assignment had something to do with politics and the government and the U.S. role in the building of the Panama Canal, but no matter how many times I read the instructions, I couldn't make my mind focus. Everything seemed to have turned upside down and spun around backward.

I flipped to a clean sheet of paper in my notebook but it stayed pristine white, untainted. When my butt got too cold, I stood and started kicking at a crack in the concrete until Jess came out.

"How'd it go?" I searched her face.

She shrugged. "Good enough, I guess. They said I'm further along on this little journey than I thought."

"What do you mean *further along*?"

She rolled her eyes. "I don't know. They don't know what they're talking about. I mean, I guess this pregnancy thing usually lasts nine months."

"That's traditionally the case."

"Well, they said I'm already over four months along. Or whatever."

"So your due date is…" I calculated in my head but wanted to hear it from her.

"May. Right before graduation." There was no hiding it now. "I'm going to have to tell my dad. There won't be any *see ya* after graduation then leaving before the baby comes." She kicked at the same crack I'd been kicking. "Dammit." Her eyes were bright and round. "What am I going to do? That bastard." I didn't know if she meant Paul or her dad. Maybe both. Then she burst into tears. "Shit. Shit. Shit." The heel of her boot kicked at the concrete with each word. "Oh my God, Rowan, what am I going to do?"

As much as I wanted to have the answers, I didn't. "Did they talk to you about options?"

"Yeah." She strung the word out in a long breath. "Adoption. Which means I have the baby and give it away. Still no hiding that. Or abortion, but they said that's not a good option because I'm so far along and I'm not eighteen so I'd need permission."

A woman with hair so long it fell past her waist was walking toward us with the lumbering walk of the heavily pregnant. We could hear her raspy, struggling breath before she even got to the entrance. Her stomach was so large and round surely she would topple forward any minute.

I pulled open the door for her.

"Thanks," she whispered, as if the weight of the baby had taken even her voice.

As the door shut behind her Jess said, "So that's what I have to look forward to the rest of my senior year? People's pity as I walk down the hallways like an enormous fool? Their judgment? And I have no idea how I'm going to pay for this. Go on welfare or something, I guess."

"What about Paul? I mean, he should help out in some way."

She wiped her eye with her shirtsleeve. "He's changed his cell phone number. I don't know how to get ahold of him." She crumpled over into a ball on the sidewalk, her back shaking under my hand.

I would kill Paul if I had the chance. How dare he do this? Maybe I'd try to find him. Maybe he would come to his senses and come back to help her. It was his child as well.

But those weren't words to say right now.

"Is everything okay out here?" The nurse who had taken Jess back to the exam room popped her head out the door. "Jessica? Do you want to come back inside for a bit? We can have one of the nurses talk to you some more."

Without looking up, she shook her head.

"I'll take her home," I said. "Thank you."

"Okay. Jessica, take care of yourself and call one of those numbers if you need anything."

"What numbers?" I asked.

Jess stood and dusted off her knees. "Just hotline numbers for this or that. Who knows?" She sighed—a heavy, shaking sound.

"Let's go." I stepped off the sidewalk.

"Okay."

On the way home, Jess closed her eyes. I couldn't tell if she was asleep or not, but at least she wasn't crying. I wished there was someone to talk to, to help give me answers. But there wasn't anyone I could think of.

THE ANDERSON'S house was black when we got back. I rushed inside to turn on some lights for the animals and then locked the door behind Jess. She dropped onto the couch without a word while I let the dogs outside and fed Scout.

I hadn't told her about seeing my dad, or seeing Trina doing drugs, or not wanting to talk to Mike. She had enough to think about without worrying about me.

She didn't say anything about dinner, and I didn't feel like eating either, so I turned on the television and pet Levi's head.

After just a few minutes, Jess stood. "I think I'll go on to bed. I'm exhausted."

"Okay."

She forced a smile and stumbled to the stairs. Levi followed her and they both stopped at the bottom. "Rowan?" She turned to me.

I glanced at her over the back of the couch. "Yeah?"

"Thank you."

I smiled. She forced another one and when her lip started to tremor, she rushed up the stairs. Levi sat there long after the door to my room *clicked* shut, like he was listening for sobs or snores. If he heard sobs, I had no doubt he would've gone up the stairs after her.

"It's okay, boy. She'll be okay." He looked at me, unblinking, like he knew I was lying; that no one knew if she would be okay. But finally he trotted over to me. Delilah lay at one end of the couch and watched Levi with sleepy, weary eyes, her flat, pink tongue hanging out from her lips. When Levi hopped up beside me, she lumbered to her feet and moved toward us, her weight pushing into the cushions.

She pushed at Levi until he moved to my other side and soon I was sandwiched in-between two hot, furry bodies. They not only warmed my cold skin, but also my cold heart. Moments later, I pulled out my phone and called Mike.

"Hey, Rowan! I was going to call you." It was so nice to hear his voice I closed my eyes and let it wash over me.

"How did the tournament go?" My words were bright, like little bursts from a sparkler.

I think he answered but his voice was drowned out by the noise in the background.

"You have to speak up," I said. "I can't hear you."

"Oh, sorry!" he yelled into the phone. "Just a minute."

The noise soared louder then suddenly dropped off completely. "Is that better?"

"Where are you? It sounds like you're at a party."

"I am. We won the tournament and one guy decided to have his fraternity throw us a party."

For some reason the world in front of me turned cloudy and overcast.

"Oh."

"Yeah. It was a great game. I scored a goal, and we beat the other team by two goals."

"Congratulations. That's great." If he noticed that my words sounded hollow, he didn't say—probably because he started talking to someone who walked into the room instead of listening to me. It was a girl's voice, and I fought to temper the tone of my words. "Who is that?"

"Oh, just JJ's girlfriend. She's pretty cool. She had too much to drink, though, and wanted a place to lie down."

"Are you in a bedroom?" Little prickly jabs flooded over my skin. Maybe they came from inside me. Maybe they didn't. Who knew? Mike was in a bedroom, away at college, with a girl who was drunk.

"Is she there now?"

"Yeah. I'm sitting in a chair, and she's lying on the bed. I think she's passed out."

"No, I'm not," the girl called out.

It took everything I had not to hang up on him. It didn't sound like he was doing anything wrong, but something felt wrong. Very wrong indeed.

"You're obviously busy. I'll talk to you later."

"Hey, wait a minute."

My hand paused mid-pet on Levi's head.

"My parents are going to stay another couple of days if that's okay with you." Darkness seemed to descend all around me. "Mom is going to call you later to talk to you about it."

I swallowed. "No. That's fine. Tell her not to call." Suddenly, she was the last person I wanted to talk to, next to her son. "Tell her that's fine. Jess is here with me. We are okay."

"Okay. I'll let her know. Hey, listen. I gotta run. I'm going to give Natalie the room to herself. She's not looking too hot. I'll call you tomorrow."

An influx of noise drowned out anything else he might want to say, or anything I might want to say to him. It sounded like the entire party had just moved into that bedroom. I hung up the phone without another word. Then I curled around my dog, Delilah's warmth at my back, and let the hollowness surround me.

chapter eleven

THE NEXT morning I was in the kitchen filling my water bottle when Jess walked in. My backpack slid from my grasp and fell to the floor. "Um, Jess, what are you doing?"

She sauntered into the room, twirled in front of me, and then struck a runway pose, all hips and arms and smiles. She was wearing a matching pink plaid skirt and jacket with a silk cream blouse, nude panty hose, and pumps. Her hair was pulled back into a severe ponytail; it looked like a shiny, black ball.

"If I'm going to have a kid," she struck another pose, "then I might as well start looking like a mom."

"You can't wear that," I sputtered. I'd seen that exact outfit on Mrs. Anderson the last time we went to church. "She wears those clothes."

"There's a ton of stuff in her closet. She'll never notice."

"But…but she will! She wore it two weeks ago!"

Jess shrugged and twirled again. "Looks like we'll have to go shopping. I need some new clothes."

"Okay…just don't wear Mrs. A.'s in the meantime. Have you grown out of your clothes already?"

"No. But you know…" She took the carton of milk out of the refrigerator. "I don't know. Trying something new, I guess."

"Okay. Except you can't try something new with her clothes."

She poured the milk into a tall glass, filling it all the way to the top so she had to bend over and sip it before she could pick it up.

"Are you wearing her makeup, too?"

Jess normally wore red lipstick and thick eyeliner behind her glasses. Today she had on soft peach lipstick, a light swipe of blush, and her contact lenses.

She shrugged and lifted the glass. "I tried some on. You don't have any so I had to go into her bathroom. She's got tons of stuff! Not usually my style, but so much she won't miss it."

"Jess." I sighed. "Leave her stuff alone. You shouldn't even go in there. Are you planning to come to school today or are you taking the day off again?"

She put the milk back in the refrigerator. "Maybe I'll go to the grocery store today. I'm starving. Seriously, I need some pickles or something."

"And ice cream?"

She made a sour face. "Actually both sound awful. I'd love some fruit, though. Something melon-y."

"What about school?"

She met my gaze. "Why? Why would I continue?"

My mouth fell open. "Are you serious?"

"Ro, what does it matter? I'm not going to college like you. I'm not going to be no veterinarian."

"Jess, get serious. You are half a year away from graduation. You don't know you won't ever want to go to college. You might change your mind."

I could tell she was trying not to unravel. She pulled at a piece of hair and watched me.

"Come on. Go change. We'll take it one day at a time."

She fell into the chair and shook her head. Her lips moved but no sound came out of her mouth.

I sat in the chair beside her. "Jess?"

"What am I going to do when I start showing? What am I going to do with a baby?" Her shoulders hunched. "Everyone is going to know I got knocked up and the baby's father left me." She paused then whispered, "Damn him."

Damn him was right. Hatred tore through me as I watched my best friend fall apart.

"What's going to happen to me? To us?" She wiped her nose with her hand then closed her eyes.

I rubbed her shoulder. "We'll figure it out." I neglected to say I had no idea how we would do that.

Would we figure it out? There was little doubt her dad would kick her out of the house. Then where would she go? Especially with a baby?

"Have you thought about…you know, adoption?"

Her eyes were glazed over and I wasn't sure she heard me. After several minutes her lips moved. It took another moment before any words came out. "I guess. I mean, yeah. I've thought about it. I keep thinking Paul is going to return and whisk us away."

My heart shattered into a thousand pieces as I watched her, lost and afraid, stare out the Anderson's back window. From the look on her face it was a dark place where her thoughts hovered.

"Have you heard from him?"

She shook her head.

"Maybe you should start thinking about adoption. In case…" I couldn't bring myself to say the words.

"In case he never returns."

My heart broke a little bit more when she said those words.

I glanced at the clock, desperate to pull us out of the place we were in. "Come on. Let's go to school. You can't stay here alone today." I stood and held out my hand.

She shook her head. "I can't. I just can't." She stood and walked out of the room, Mrs. Anderson's shoes clacking along the way.

I stayed at the table, staring out at the backyard until I realized I was going to be late again. I ran out the door and made it a few minutes after the tardy bell.

"HI, ROWAN!" Trina popped up beside me, all hips and smiles and perfume. She bounced up and down on the balls of her feet like a kid in a candy store.

"What do you want, Trina?" I yanked my English book out of my locker.

"Just to chat." She leaned toward me. "You seen Dad yet?"

"Why?" I snapped.

She shrugged and twirled her hair around her finger. "He's dying, you know." If she'd just been given a bag of lollipops, she wouldn't have sounded more excited. Her pupils were huge—the large, black masses nearly pushing out the blue around them.

"Yeah. I know." I pulled out my notebook.

"So, you should, like, really forgive him. I mean, he's harmless now. Dying and all."

"Shut up, Trina. You don't know anything."

Her smile faded to a sneer. "You're such a self-righteous bitch, Rowan. He made a mistake. What are you going to do, cut us all out of your life forever?" Her words came out in a manic rush.

"That's exactly what I'd like to do." But I wasn't sure those words were true. How would I feel a year from now, five years, fifteen? Would I start to miss my family? It was one thing to refuse to have a relationship with someone when you know they are just a few miles away. If they were dead didn't that change something?

"He's coming to dinner tonight if you want to come over. Gran said to invite you. She's always talking about how much she misses you. *Oh Rowan this* and *oh Rowan that*. She's going to put a shrine in your room. Stupid if you ask me since you left us and you know, got a new family." I don't think she took a single breath until she finished that useless string of words.

I started down the hall. "No, thanks. I'm not up for playing happy little family."

Suddenly, Trina grabbed my arm, her nails digging in through my shirtsleeve. I tried to yank away but her hand was clamped so tight, I couldn't. "Let go of me."

To my surprise, she did.

"Don't EVER touch me again."

"Oh, is that a threat? What are you going to do about it? You're losing weight again. You're about as skinny as I was when I was eight. But you're eighteen, aren't you? You couldn't hurt anything. You are a pathetic kid, stuck in a little boy's body trying to act all bad and tough and grown-up. You're such a poser. I bet you really *are* a little boy. Dad had his boy all along."

My vision turned red, and my fists clenched. "Shut up, Trina."

"I never did understand why Mike wanted you." Her huge eyes ran up and down my skinny body, and I had never felt uglier. "Especially when he could've had this." Trina lifted her shirt in the middle of the hall, exposing her pink bra with cups that were filled to the point of overflowing.

Soon chants of *oohs* and *ahhs* filled the air around us, but I didn't care. Rage tore through my body with the strength of a fire hose, and I shoved her so hard she stumbled then fell, her shirt still hiked up over her chest.

"You're just jealous because he would never want a slut like you," I spat. I turned on my heel and started down the hall, my body rigid but my insides tumbling.

Her footsteps pounded toward me. I didn't have enough time to react before she yanked a handful of my hair so hard my books went flying out of my arms and across the floor.

I screamed but she wouldn't let go of my hair, and I whipped around to grab at her face. When I felt skin, I dug my nails in until she cried out.

Within a heartbeat, her hand was up, landing a blow on my cheekbone. Pain shot through my face, but it didn't stop me. I shoved her so hard she fell onto her back again and then I was on her, fists flying into her as fast as hers were flying into me. Somehow I pulled together all of the hatred and anger and resentment I'd ever had toward my sister and used it in the weight of my punches.

Someone yanked me off her. "Rowan, stop!" Miss J. wrapped her arms around me like a vise.

Trina sat up, blood trickling from her lip. Her left eye was swollen and her face was flushed bright red.

Principal Thompson shuffled down the hall, trying to move faster than his substantial weight would allow. He leaned over Trina and helped her up. "Girls. In my office. Now."

Miss J. let go of me with a sigh. "Come see me when you're done."

My sister and I followed him into his office.

PRINCIPAL THOMPSON motioned for us to sit down, then stared at us for several minutes. His office was large with an enormous wooden desk, an equally large chair behind it, and overflowing bookshelves. The window looked out on the lawn in front of the school.

His breathing was loud like he was asthmatic. With arms crossed over his protruding belly, he said nothing. Trina's legs were crossed, and she was kicking one of her feet so fast there was no way he didn't notice. And what about her eyes? He'd have to notice that, too. But he didn't say anything about those things. Rather, he said, "Now, girls. What happened out there?"

His voice was surprisingly high-pitched for such a large man. When neither of us answered, he continued, "You've had a rough year. I get that. But that doesn't mean you can roll around on the floors of this school like animals." He looked at me. He looked at Trina. "Is something new going on?"

"No, sir," I answered, flipping my own gaze up to meet his, then quickly dropping it again.

"No," said Trina.

"This school year is almost halfway over. I don't want anything like this happening again. If the two of you are having a problem at home, or just in general, come to me or Miss Johnson."

I prayed for this lecture to be over soon, and I started biting my nails.

"I'm going to ignore what happened out there as long as it doesn't happen again. Do you understand?"

"Yes." Thank God he wasn't going to suspend us. He did not take fighting lightly.

"Yes," croaked Trina, her foot going a mile a minute.

"Rowan, you're excused."

Trina pushed to her feet at the same time but Principal Thompson motioned for her to stop. "Not you, Trina. I need another word with you."

I didn't look at her when I walked out of the room. The hallway was empty, and I was glad. I could feel the burn of embarrassment reddening my cheeks. My books were gone from the floor, and I assumed Miss J. had gathered them for me. I turned left and headed straight for her office.

"WHAT HAPPENED back there?" Miss J.'s eyes were wide and unblinking. "What is going on?"

I had never hit another person in my life. It felt so good to pummel Trina's stoned, lying, bitch face, I kind of yearned to do it again. I clenched my fingers around my arm to keep from lifting my shirtsleeve. My body was on fire with more emotions than I could handle, and I felt the old, familiar urge send my insides into a tailspin.

"Spill it," Miss J. said.

"You said you'd tell me why you were proof that if someone wanted something bad enough they couldn't let anything stand in their way. What did you mean? What happened?"

She went to the small refrigerator that sat to the side of the room, pulled out a cold diet drink, and handed it to me. "Put this on your face."

I did, wincing as the cold made my skin scream.

"Why do you want to know?" Her eyes narrowed.

"Because. I get one step forward but it's always two steps back. Always. I need some inspiration here."

The room was quiet except for the loud whir of the school's heating system. She watched me as I watched her. I could almost see her mind flipping between excuses and the truth.

Finally she said, "I was molested when I was little. By my uncle. No one believed me when I told. There." She slapped her palms on the desk.

"My God. That's awful."

"Yes. It was awful. But I survived. And here I am. I have managed to be a happy person despite what my childhood was like. That's what I want for you as well, Rowan. And I know you can do that. You are more, so much more, than your family."

"How long did it last?"

Her jaw clenched, and I wasn't sure she would answer me. "Five years."

"I'm sorry." My voice was barely louder than a whisper.

"Well, it's over and I've moved on. It took time. It took therapy, which I highly recommended for you, as you know. And it took determination not to let that identify and shape my future. I moved past it, Rowan, and so can you."

Another thirty minutes passed with us talking in low voices. Trina was barely mentioned.

When I finally got up from the chair, I felt more drained and exhausted than I had ever felt. In one hand was an excuse slip for missing class and in the other was the soda. It had grown warm against my skin but felt amazing on my dry throat. After all of that talking, I needed it.

Last year if something like this had happened, I would've run into the girls' bathroom, razor vibrating in my pocket. But this time I walked right past it to my next class. I yearned for that release except I was too depleted to give in to the urge.

Miss J. had overcome more than I could've imagined. Was I destined for a future where I kept falling over myself as I tried to stand on my own two feet? With my family and my past trailing me like a foul odor? Or was I destined to let it go? To forgive and if not forget, move beyond it?

I didn't know the answers, but I spent the rest of the day thinking and not paying one bit of attention to what my teachers said.

chapter twelve

"HEY, RO." Mike called just as I was walking to my car. It was a welcome respite to hear his voice after such a long day even if it was over the phone. "How are you?"

"Um, good." I dug through my bag until I found my keys.

"How was school?" His voice seemed foreign to me all of a sudden, as if the weird places my mind traveled today were places where he didn't exist. And now I was trying to come back into a world that had Mike in it.

"It was fine. Nothing too crazy." But that wasn't true, was it? "What are you up to?"

"Just got back from practice. It was a tough workout today. We had a new trainer that kicked our butts."

"Why do you have a new trainer?" I slid into the driver's seat and started the car.

"Coach says we're out of shape. This spring he has us in double the tournaments than any other year plus regular season games. He's determined to have us play so much soccer we play in our sleep."

We both knew what that meant, but neither of us brought it up.

"Well, you're already in great shape. I can't imagine the trainer can do too much to help you."

"Oh, you'd be surprised. The trainer's name is Rob, but he has this assistant named Suzie, and man, she really gives it to us hard."

"You have a female trainer?" And she gives it to you *hard*?

"Yeah. She graduated from the sports medicine program two years ago and is helping out on the side. She says she needs more experience."

"Why do you know so much about her?" I cringed as soon as the words came out of my mouth.

He laughed. "Cause she kicks my butt every day. She's in charge of the freshmen, and since there are only five of us on the team, there's plenty of time to talk between sets."

Plenty of time to talk, he says. Well, I was glad he had time to talk to her. He certainly didn't have time to talk to me.

"I gotta go," I said.

"What? Why?"

"I just have to go."

"Wait a minute. When do you expect to hear from the colleges? I can't remember when those letters come."

"Not yet." I tried hard not to snap.

"You don't have anything to worry about. You'll get in. Then you can be up here with me."

I pulled at my earring. "Yeah. That sounds good. Or there might be another school that offers me more financial aid. We'll just have to wait and see."

"Nah. You'll come here. I'm sure they'll offer aid. You need to be here with me."

"Why, Mike?" My voice echoed my frustration. And once the words started, I found I couldn't stop. "It's not like we see each other now. What does it matter what school I go to? You'll be so busy with soccer we'll still never see each other." Irritation colored my words.

"We could see each other more. Isn't that the point?" His own words were clipped, short.

I pinched the bridge of my nose. I didn't want to fight with him. We saw each other so rarely and hardly spoke to each other as it was. Fighting wasn't how I wanted to spend our phone conversations.

"Sorry. It's just been a long day," I said.

"Is everything okay?" His voice softened. He knew my history, and I loved that no matter what, he was always concerned about me. He usually had good reason to be.

I thought about Jess, Dad, Trina, how lonely I was. "Yeah. Everything is fine. Just a couple of things going on."

"Like what?"

Some invisible wall kept me from speaking. I wasn't sure why. It wasn't like there was anything I could say to him that would be surprising. He knew I came with a lot of issues; that was really how we'd gotten together. He had come to my rescue last spring like a knight in shining armor. I owed him honesty and openness.

So I took a deep breath, ready to force myself to launch into everything that was going on, but he started talking to someone in the background.

"Yeah, I'll be right there," he was saying.

"Do you have to go?" My heart fell to the floor.

"I do. I'll call you later, okay?"

Without waiting for me to respond, he said, "Love ya," and hung up. I sat in the parking lot for a long time, thinking, and trying not to think all at the same time.

I DROVE toward the interstate. The animal shelter was in the opposite direction, but I wasn't due at work until five o'clock. I hadn't been on the schedule for a few days and it would be nice to be back among the animals. Before I went to work, I had just enough time to get to the small college the next town over, the one Miss J. encouraged me to apply to, and the one I doubted I had much chance of being accepted into.

To get there, I had to drive a winding road that circled up a mountain like a snake. It would be difficult to get to school if the weather was bad, but that couldn't be a concern now. I might not even like this college despite Miss J.'s conviction that I would.

Finally, the campus loomed before me. It was a small school, but it seemed huge to me. There was a large brick arch that read *Berkeley Mountain College* in black iron letters right at the peak. I drove through it and was on the campus. There was an empty parking space so I pulled into it, taking a minute in my warm car to look around.

From this vantage point there were six buildings, all brick, and all looked to be four stories high. There were tall, black iron signs placed around to point students and visitors into the direction they wanted. Student union? Straight ahead. Library? Make a right. Biology lab? Go left.

There was a large, flat grassy area to my left that I would walk through each time I headed to class since all the parking seemed to be on the right side of the campus. In the middle of this was a water fountain, now off for the winter. Several students sat along the short wall that enclosed it even though the day was cold.

Other students walked between the buildings across the wide green lawn, or sat on benches huddled in their winter coats. Miss J. had tried several times to get me to visit this college, but I had never given it much credibility. For one thing, it only took students who were smarter than me and who had far more money than I did. And I didn't think a liberal arts college would have a good enough biology program to get me into veterinary school. Miss J. said that it was a stellar program, though, and even offered classes on zoology and animal nutrition. Finally, it wasn't the university where Mike was. Suddenly, though, it seemed like a possibility…

I stepped out of the car. I put my hands in my pockets as I veered left toward the biology building. Groups of students piled out of the main entrance, backpacks slung over shoulders.

"That lecture was amazing."

"I love how eccentric she is, always carrying those little umbrellas."

"I'm going to sign up for that extra lab. What about you?"

Their voices faded into the afternoon as they walked away. I changed my mind mid-stride and followed them at a distance, close enough to hear their voices, but not what they were saying as they headed toward the student union. When we came to the entrance, they walked in. I stopped near a group of students standing around a guy playing the guitar.

He sat on the highest of the five long steps that led into the building, off toward the side so people could get past if they wanted to. I stopped at the bottom and leaned against the railing, listening.

He was playing an eclectic mix of familiar bluegrass and what sounded like Spanish guitar, similar to what I had heard in class last semester. It was by far the most beautiful sound I'd ever heard. If I could listen to music like this every moment of my life, surely there would be no pain—no past, present, or future. Just the beauty of the music.

I didn't know enough about guitars to describe the music he was making. The only thing I could think was that it was mesmerizing. Haunting. Insanely beautiful.

If there was tension in my body it was gone by the time he stopped playing. My eyes were closed, and when I opened them he was watching me from the bluest eyes I'd ever seen. My cheeks were covered in tears, and I looked away as the group started to leave.

I tensed and turned my back when he started coming down the steps.

Please don't stop and talk to me. Please.

I felt him hovering behind me, just to the side of my right shoulder. I turned and glanced up. "I'm sorry. That was amazing," I choked. Then I laughed, wiping my eyes. "I'm sorry."

"Don't apologize. Music should move you. I'm just glad it was my music that did."

Warmth spread across my cheeks. "You are very talented."

"I practice…a lot."

"I can tell." I wiped at my cheeks and took a closer look at him. He was tall, wearing worn-out jeans with a rip at one knee. His hair was light brown, hanging to his shoulders in waves.

"Shane." He reached out his hand.

"Rowan." His fingers closed around mine.

"Nice to meet you, Rowan. Are you a student here?"

I shook my head, completely ignorant of the freezing air around me. "I'm a senior in high school."

"Cool. You think you might come here next year? It's a great school."

"What year are you?"

"This is my third year. I'm a music major with a minor in English. I love to play guitar, and I love to read. So I merged the two, making me destined for a life of petty crime and menial jobs." He laughed softly.

"Well, you have to do what you love."

"Yeah, no matter what bleak future it lays out before you. What will you study?"

"Biology. My plan is to go on to veterinary school."

He nodded, his expression showing he was impressed or at least trying to act like he was. "That's great. I love animals. I have a golden retriever named Barney back home. Best dog ever."

"I have a dog. Levi. And a cat named Scout."

"From *To Kill a Mockingbird*, I assume?" His voice was like butterscotch—smooth and velvety.

"Yep. I like to read, too." I glanced at my watch. "I need to go. It was nice to meet you, Shane." Without thinking, I climbed up two steps to put myself eye level with him. His brows pursed as he studied my face.

"Is there something wrong?" I asked, rubbing my chin.

"You have a bruise on your cheek. Looks like you just got into a fight. Bad day at school?"

I touched the bruise. Why hadn't I covered it up? "No. It was just an accident," I lied. "It's fine. Doesn't hurt at all."

He seemed to believe me; if he didn't, he hid it really well. "Well, it's nice to meet you, Rowan. Why don't you look me up next time you're here, and I'll show you around. It may not look like much, but there is a surprising amount this school offers."

"I'd like that." And I chose not to acknowledge exactly how good that sounded.

"Shane!" called a girl, running up with another guy on her heels. "Ready?"

"Hey. Tara, John, this is Rowan. She may come here next year. Rowan, Tara and John."

Tara was a plain-looking girl with reddish-orange hair. She flashed a huge smile when she shook my hand. She seemed so genuine, I found myself smiling back. John, hands shoved in his pockets, nodded. "Hey," he said. "Nice to meet you."

"Nice to meet you, too," I said.

"I'll give you my number." Shane pulled out a piece of paper from his backpack and wrote his name and phone number across it. He folded it and handed it to me. His fingers grazed my skin, and I bit my lip. What was wrong with me? Was I so starved for attention that a little conversation with a guy made me blush? Guess so.

"Thanks. Well, bye everyone." I flew down the sidewalk suddenly too embarrassed to look at him.

"Rowan!" he called.

I turned and looked over my shoulder. There were several yards between us, and I hoped they couldn't see the new flush on my cheeks. Or maybe they would think it was the cold. I knew it wasn't.

"Yeah?"

"Put some ice on that bruise."

I nodded and darted toward my car. My hands didn't stop shaking until I parked the car at the animal shelter.

I MADE it to work with five minutes to spare. Janie was on the phone when I walked in and waved to me from behind the desk. My boss was older than my mom, in her mid-fifties if I had to guess, with long, graying hair that hung in frizzy curls to her waist. The skin on her face was wrinkled and perpetually tanned, but it only made her look happy, like she'd led a life well-lived.

Her wardrobe consisted of blue jean overalls, worn and faded, with a flannel shirt underneath. Today's top was purple and brown, the edges around the sleeves frayed. Her light beige boots had scuff marks across the toe.

I was pretty sure Janie had a girlfriend, something foreign in this small town. Instead of saying she had a girlfriend, though, she called her a *roommate*. I'd met her *roommate*, Angel, before. She often came into the shelter a half hour before closing when she was done with work. I'd seen enough stolen kisses to confirm my suspicion, not that it mattered to me.

Angel was one of the smartest people I'd ever met. When I couldn't figure out a chemistry problem one evening when the shelter was quiet, she not only told me the correct answer but explained it in a way that was clearer than anything my teacher had ever said. I think she was a professor or a lawyer. I wasn't entirely sure and had never wanted to ask, but she was my go-to person with any homework questions.

I mouthed to Janie that I was going into the back room. I needed to clean the cages. The first room I came to was the dog room. The animals knew me by my voice so I always started talking to them as soon as I walked through the door. I greeted each one, cage by cage, checking that their bowls were filled. Then I changed any soiled bedding and swept the floors. After those chores were done, I took the dogs out, one by one, for a walk behind the shelter.

Even in the deepest of cold the dogs always wanted to play. In the fenced yard they would chase balls, Frisbees, and play tug-of-war. If the dog was well-socialized, I could bring more than one out at a time, and they would chase each other.

For the cats, I took several minutes to pet each one. Some I took out of their cages to let them roam around and stretch their legs. The ones that let me I cuddled close to my heart as I stroked their heads, trying to make them feel loved.

It wasn't always easy to feel loved, especially when it seemed like no one wanted you. I knew how that felt to the core of my very being. And if I could help these sweet animals feel a little better about their lives, I would.

FOUR HOURS later, at closing time, Janie found me in the back room with a cat in my lap, one in my arms and a couple of them lying on the floor around me.

"Rowan? You're not supposed to take all of those animals out." Janie tilted her head to the side, her expression more bewilderment than anger.

"I know. But I could tell they needed a little more love tonight. Is that okay? When one of them needs just a little extra love to give them that?" I bent my head to nuzzle the tabby cat in my arms. It was new to our shelter, and I could feel its ribs every time I brushed my fingers over its fur.

Janie sighed and said, "Yes. I suppose it's okay." Instead of leaving the room, she walked over and stared down at me. Then she sat, pulling the cat from my lap and putting it into hers. Soon the cat's purr filled the room and another one moved from my side to hers. "It's okay indeed." Her face lit as the cat swatted at a loose thread on her overalls.

chapter thirteen

WHEN I got home it was past nine o'clock, and Jess was asleep on the couch. I put a blanket over her then went into the kitchen. I stared into the refrigerator that Jess filled but shut the door without getting anything. Instead, I poured a glass of water and went upstairs to find my journal. Before I sat on my bed beside Scout, I pulled a framed picture of Mike and me off my dresser and looked at it.

The picture was taken last May when we went to the Prom. Mike was dressed in a black tuxedo and I was wearing a mint green Prom dress his mom had helped me pick out. His arm was thrown over my shoulders. I was so closely snuggled into his side, half of my body was hidden. It was the best night of my entire life and I smiled at the memories, at his handsome face staring back at me.

My phone rang and when I saw it was Mrs. Anderson, I let it go to voicemail. I knew that she was going to tell me they were staying longer, but I listened to the message anyway.

Hi, Rowan. It's Mike's mom. Mr. Anderson and I will be home tomorrow night. If you need me for anything just give me a call. I hope school is going well.

I deleted the message and brought the picture close to my face, staring at his eyes. Those green orbs of his always made me melt like chocolate. I missed him, and his eyes, with a yearning that made me choke.

I'd had a crush on Mike long before we started dating last year. But he'd had a girlfriend. They broke up and soon after we were paired for a biology project. He saw something in me that kept him by my side through all the madness, and had him opening the doors to his home and his family.

Mike was my savior. He had stood by my side throughout some of the worst moments of my life and had never once judged me. I smiled at the picture as I laid it down on the bed in front of me. For this one moment, my heart released its hold on the loneliness and let a sliver of contentment come in. No matter what, Mike had changed my life. I would still be at home if it weren't for him, slowly dying under the weight of my family.

I uncapped the pen.

> *A moment*
> *One moment*
> *Can change everything.*
> *A person*
> *One person*
> *Can be the cause.*
> *A touch*
> *One touch*
> *Can make us whole again.*

Somehow, around the third or fourth line, Mike's image had slipped away and in its place was Shane's. No matter how hard I stared at Mike's picture, he suddenly seemed like a stranger; a thing of the past. I slammed the journal shut and nearly drowned in my own disbelief.

AN HOUR or so later, I left my bedroom with Scout cradled against my chest and went downstairs to check on Jess. The couch was empty, the blanket crumpled up on the floor.

"Jess?"

No answer. I walked into the kitchen expecting to see her sitting at the table eating. But she wasn't there. It was too cold for her to be outside, but I looked out the back window anyway. She wasn't there either.

I walked to the front door and saw that it was still dead bolted. "Jess!"

"What?"

It sounded like she was somewhere upstairs.

"What are you doing?" I ran up the stairs, Levi on my heels. I let Scout down, and she darted into my room.

"Jess?" I opened the door to Mr. and Mrs. Anderson's bedroom. "What are you doing in here?" I followed the sound of something being tossed around.

"In the closet," she said.

I walked in and found Jess sitting on the floor of Mrs. Anderson's closet, piles of clothes lying around her.

"What the hell?"

She shrugged and lifted a silk blouse off the floor. "Just thought I'd look through her clothes again. What's wrong with that?"

"What's wrong with that? You can't be in here!" My voice was shrill.

"Why not?" she demanded, squeezing the shirt in her fist. "I need some new clothes. I can't afford to go to the thrift store to buy anything."

"You can't take these. You're kidding me, right?"

"No. She won't miss them. And I have to save my money." Jess' voice was rising, bordering on hysteria. "I can't afford maternity clothes." She started to hyperventilate. "Even if I can find someone to adopt this baby, I can't afford to even get to that point!"

"Jess?" I watched her as closely as someone watches a foaming-mouthed rottweiler.

"What?" she screamed, her words coming out in hiccups. "I can't do this, Rowan! I can't!"

I fell to my knees beside her and touched her shoulder.

"I can't do this," she repeated.

"You can."

She buried her face in her hands. I couldn't imagine what was going on in her head. Finally, she spoke. "I want to keep it, Rowan."

"The baby?"

She nodded and lowered her hands. Her eyes were terrified. "I want to keep it. Can I?"

"You're asking *me?*" Why would she ask me that?

"Rowan, can I handle it? Can I raise this baby? I need you to tell me I can. You're my best friend. If you tell me I can do it, then I know I can."

Several thoughts flashed through my mind. Was it up to me to help sway her decision? Or was it up to her and her alone?

She placed a hand on her just-starting-to-round stomach.

I felt like I was flinging us both off the edge of a cliff, but I said it anyway. "You can handle it. I know you can." I was surprised to hear confidence in my voice. Maybe I *did* believe she could do it.

She blinked several times. "You think so?"

"I know so." I smiled.

Several quiet seconds passed as I looked around at Mrs. Anderson's clothes. "I got into a fight at school today," I said, breaking the silence.

"What?" Her eyes widened. "Oh my God, with who?"

"Trina."

Jess rolled her eyes. "That bitch. I hope you gave it to her good."

"I don't know. I'm so tired of her. Maybe I should go away to the university with Mike, get as far away from here as possible."

"You're thinking of *not* going to the same school as Mike? I thought that was a done deal." She rubbed her tummy in small circles.

"I don't know. There's that school, Berkeley Mountain College. It's supposed to be good."

"Hmm." Jess eyed me as I put a blouse on a hanger. "When did you change your mind?"

"Well, I didn't. I'm just keeping my options open."

She unnerved me with her sounds and her eyes. I knew what would turn her focus to something else. "Let's go order something to eat."

At the mention of food, Jess jumped up, stepping over Mrs. Anderson's expensive shoes, and dashed downstairs as if the conversation we'd had over the last half hour didn't happen. I followed her even though food was the last thing on my mind.

She got on the phone and called the only Chinese restaurant in our area that also happened to deliver. While she was talking, my cell rang. When I saw that it was Mike, I ran to my room to talk to him in private.

"Hey, Ro."

"Hey." I lay down on my bed and put my feet up against the wall.

"I feel like we haven't had a chance to talk since I left."

I fought to keep my voice upbeat. It was becoming harder and harder to swallow the bite of my words. It seemed like even our phone conversations were becoming almost an inconvenience.

"Yeah. I know." I sighed.

"So, what have you and Jess been up to? How's Paul?"

I couldn't help but laugh, though there was nothing funny about it. Mike really was in the dark. I forced my mouth to open and willed words to come out, trying to convince myself that sharing my life was what I was supposed to do. "He went to Colorado to find a job, and I'm not sure he's coming back."

"Not coming back? You're kidding. Why wouldn't he come back?"

"Well..." I swatted at a piece of dust floating down from the ceiling. "I'm not sure."

"What's going on? Is something wrong?"

"Yeah. You could say that." I clenched my teeth. I would tell him what was going on. It was the right thing to do.

"Spill it," he commanded. It was quiet on his end, which hopefully meant I had his undivided attention. "Rowan? What's wrong? Please tell me."

And in those three words, I heard the old Mike come out; the one who cared so deeply about my well-being that he would have me move in with him and his family even after only a month of dating. My heart thawed, and I launched into everything that was going on—Paul, Jess' pregnancy…

I had his attention for a full ten minutes before the slamming of a door and the deep, gruff voices of his fraternity brothers rang through the phone. It was longer than I expected, though, and as I hung up the phone I felt better than I had in a while. I ran downstairs just as the Chinese food arrived.

"How's Mike?" Jess asked. She was dressed, thankfully, in her own clothes—a short black skirt so tight I could see the slightest rounding of her stomach, black tights, and a gray, off-the-shoulder sweater. Her skin was clearer than I'd ever seen it, and her black hair was combed and held back with a headband, even though that didn't mask the striking blonde roots.

She must've noticed me staring because she said, "Prenatal vitamins or whatever." She waved a hand in the air then snapped her fingers. "You should try them! They're amazing for hair and nails." She shoved her fingernails, for once without polish, in my face.

"They're very nice." I pushed the end of one of her nails. "Wow. It doesn't bend at all."

"I know. Those vitamins are amazing. I should sell them on the black market." She snickered as she went to the refrigerator. "I'm starving." She grabbed a soda and plopped down at the table. "So, answer my question. How's Mike?"

"He's good." I dumped some food on my plate then used my fork to move it around, making small piles of the brownish noodles. Jess shoveled spoonfuls of it into her mouth.

"Aren't you supposed to be nauseated or something? Have an aversion to food? Morning sickness," I glanced at the clock, "even though it's not…morning."

She couldn't answer because her mouth was full, but she gave me a shrug that clearly told me to mind my own business. I busted out laughing and she smiled, food stuck in her teeth.

"You don't get to talk to him much, do you?" she asked after she took a long drink.

"No. I guess I don't." I stopped the fork full of food as I lifted it to my mouth. I really hadn't wanted it anyway.

"Is it worth it?"

My fork fell to the plate with a clang. "Is what worth it?"

"This." She waved her hand through the air. "This relationship. Don't get me wrong." She took another large bite. "I like Mike." Her words were muffled by food. "He was amazing last year. And Mrs. A.? I mean, I wish she were my mom. But, you know. He's so far away." She swallowed.

I wasn't sure where this conversation was going, but I could feel my stomach weaving into a knot. This wasn't a talk I wanted to have…mostly because I wasn't prepared to have it with myself.

"But you're young," she continued. "You're hot. Do you really want to go off to college with a boyfriend? Even if you end up at the same school as him?"

The thought of not having Mike in my life was probably the worst thing I could possibly imagine. He *was* my life, my anchor, my *Mike*. I shoved the plate away.

Jess' eyes, which I expected to widen at my reaction, watched me, calm, patient. "I know you probably don't want to talk about this, but don't you think you need to?" She paused then continued, "Is it worth it?"

I shot up from the table, knocking over my chair onto its back. "Rowan?"

I was out of the kitchen and up the stairs before she could say anything else. Her concern should not have bothered me. She was my best friend asking about my boyfriend. But it was too much, leaving me with a sinking, suffocating feeling that I was afraid I would never shake.

THE NEXT day I sat in Miss J.'s office, my legs restless; my soul restless. "Any word?"

"Rowan, slow down. You won't hear anything until at least February. We just talked about this, did we not?"

"I'm just ready to move on, I guess."

"Uh-huh. Is something else going on?"

"I went by that college the other day, Berkeley."

"Well, what did you think?" She stapled papers together and filed them in the cabinet.

"It was…really cool. I think I liked it."

Miss J. nodded. "I'm glad you decided to apply there. I know you wanted to leave this area, even go to the university where Mike is. But this college is small and has a very good reputation. You have to go through undergrad before you can go on to veterinary school, so as long as you pick a good college that will give you all the classes you need, you'll be well prepared for that next step."

I was only half listening. Instead, I heard the musical notes of guitar strings.

"Rowan?"

"Hmm?"

"Why are you blushing?"

I slouched in the seat. "I'm not blushing."

She chuckled. "Oh, but you are."

I shook my head and stood. "I can't be late. I may be waiting to hear from colleges, but I'm still in high school."

"That you are, Rowan. That you are."

I left her office with my cheeks warm. When I slid into the girls' bathroom, I saw that they were flaming red, as was my neck.

"ROWAN, YOU'VE been here for several months now." Janie stood on the other side of a dog cage, her long, gray hair held back from her face by a headband. Her reading glasses were nestled on the tip of her nose.

Inside the wire box was a tiny mutt that came to the shelter two weeks ago, starved, half-dead, and terrified. He huddled in a corner of the cage on a fluffy towel and had yet to show any response other than fear. We kept our voices soft as we spoke so we didn't scare him.

"I have. Since June. And I love it. There is nowhere else I'd rather be." I glanced down at the little dog who we'd named Charley-bear because he looked like a bear cub.

"You're doing a great job. Which brings me to a question I've wanted to ask you."

"Okay."

"I want you to become the assistant manager."

"What?" My voice rose and the little dog started to shake. I dropped to a whisper. "Really?"

She smiled, the small gap between her front teeth on perfect display. "I don't think there is anyone better suited than you."

"Wow, that's amazing. I'd love to. Um, what does that mean exactly?"

I put a finger through the grate and touched his velvety side. He was tense and shaking, but I kept my touch light.

"It means that you'll need to work about twenty hours a week, more than you do now. I know you have another semester of school and those hours can be in the evenings, and if you work two full days on the weekends, you can make the time.

"You'll also be in charge when I'm not here. You can take in animals, adopt them out, anything I do that you feel comfortable with. You'll be in charge of the volunteers when I'm not here as well."

Excitement bubbled through my blood.

"And you'll get paid more, too."

"I will?" That was just an added bonus. I could get new tires on my old car. The extra money would help pay for college. I'd still need help with the cost even if I got financial aid. "Janie, I'd love to. I mean, I can't thank you enough. You don't know how much I needed this. I'll do a good job. I promise."

She laid her hand on mine. "I know you will. This is why I asked." She smiled and my face lit up with a wide smile in return.

chapter fourteen

POSSIBILITIES. THAT was what this promotion bought me. I wasn't a person who had a lot of those. It was almost a word whose meaning I didn't clearly understand. The day I was born to parents like mine was the day that possibilities took on an elusive meaning.

But now I had them—these unattainable possibilities. The salary increase wasn't huge, but it was a huge help. The hours were going to be difficult, but maybe I could finally take Miss J.'s advice and let up on the manic schoolwork pace I'd set my freshman year.

It meant that the financial aid colleges offered me didn't have to be a deal breaker. Well, that wasn't entirely true, but it did give me some breathing room.

I nearly skipped through the door to the shelter and barely felt the cold air that blew across my skin. Assistant manager? The sound of that sent goose bumps up and down my arms completely unrelated to the freezing temperature outside. I even started humming, but stopped with a jolt when I saw my dad standing by a bench that sat outside of the door.

He said nothing as I walked toward him. He watched me, unblinking.

"Hi," I said.

He nodded.

"Did you want to see me?"

"Can we talk?" His voice sounded strained, forced. It was a surprisingly hospitable question coming from a man like him.

"Sure. I guess. Isn't it too cold for you out here? Would you like to go somewhere else?"

"I'm fine. Is this where you work now?"

"Yeah. I've been here for months. I, uh, just got promoted to assistant manager." Sharing personal information with him was something I couldn't remember ever doing voluntarily. It felt foreign, strange…nice. If he was surprised, it didn't show on his face.

"When did you stop working for Dan?"

I shuddered. I had been working for Dan at his used car lot when everything happened last year. He became, at least in my mind, a quick fix for my problems. I had even gone so far as to ask him to marry me. I didn't like to think about him, though he was for the most part an innocent bystander.

"Right after you left. I haven't seen him since."

"You were always good with animals." His monotone words belied his compliment.

Sickness oozed out of his pores so strong I could almost feel it, smell it. Even if he hadn't said he had cancer there would be no doubting it. The color of his skin had grayed, making him look like a living ghost.

"Thank you. That's…kind of you to say."

"I see your face is bruised."

I touched the sensitive skin.

"Trina told me what happened. I don't want the two of you girls fighting."

I kicked at a pinecone that was lying on the sidewalk. Did she tell him she was high on drugs at the time?

"You're all each other has. You hear me?"

I nodded and pushed my hands in my pockets, wondering if her face was bruised, too. I hadn't seen her since our fight and despite his words I didn't care if I ever did again.

But then he started to cough and pulled out a handkerchief. When he removed it from his mouth, there were patches of blood tainting the white cloth.

"Oh my God, Dad." Without thinking, I reached out and put a hand on his arm. His eyes shot up to meet mine, and I yanked my hand away. There were no caresses of affection between us; no hugs, certainly no kisses on the head. What made me reach out and touch him, I could never say. Other than he seemed so fragile at that moment; so *dying* right in front of me.

I'm not sure if I imagined it or not, but I think he nodded. Or if he didn't, he didn't jerk away when I put my hand back.

We stood there for several moments, staring down at the sight of my hand on his arm.

"Um, how long have you been coughing up blood?"

He shoved the handkerchief into his pocket. "A while. It's getting worse." His eyes settled on mine. "That's why I'm here."

My insides clamped into a tight, painful ball. *Don't say it. Don't say it. I can't handle it if you say it.*

"I don't think it'll be much longer now and neither do the doctors. The first estimate was too…generous."

He said it. I bit my lip to keep my eyes from tearing. It didn't work.

"They want me to go into hospice care."

I nodded and couldn't stop the tears. They rolled down my cheeks like droplets of rain.

"It's time to go. I'm ready. This life has proven to be one disappointment after another."

I started to sob because *I* was one of those disappointments that he was referring to. He knew it and I knew it. He'd never wanted Mom, and he'd certainly never wanted me.

As if reading my thoughts, he said, "You and Trina don't fall into that category. You especially, Rowan. You…you are a good girl. You're going to do all right."

Those words sent me into a tailspin. Time passed with my hand on his arm, my head on my hand, and sobs racking through my body. At some point I felt the warm pressure of his hand on the back of my head.

Janie walked out. "Rowan? Are you okay?" Her footsteps were heavy on the concrete. She stopped in front of us, frowning. She stared at my dad as she handed me a tissue from her large bag.

"Janie..." I sniffed. "This is my..."

Dad held out his hand. "I'm her father, Jack Slone."

"Hello." Janie shook his hand. "It's nice to meet you. I'm Janie Shue, manager of the shelter."

Dad nodded.

"Well, I've closed up. Rowan, do you need anything else?" She stared at me hard. I could tell she was trying to find out if everything was okay, if she could leave.

I cleared my throat. "I'm just going to talk to my dad a couple more minutes then head out."

"Okay. I'll see you tomorrow after school. Call me if you need anything."

Her eyes searched our faces for a clue. If I could explain, I would. But I wasn't even sure what to say. There was so much more than just my dad dying. So very much more.

TEN MINUTES later, Dad was in the front seat of my car and we were driving toward his friend's house on the outskirts of town. Ron lived in a trailer park, his home halfway down on the right. There was a shiny red pickup truck in his dirt driveway that looked brand new.

"Nice truck," I said as I pulled in.

"Yeah. He spends his money on trucks instead of his house."

I could see what Dad meant. There were several patches of rust along the trailer's side and the screen door hung off the hinges.

Dad opened the door. "I could use a ride to the hospice. They are expecting me tomorrow." His voice was hoarse as if he had a sore throat. He didn't look at me.

At first I didn't realize he was asking for a favor. When I did, I was so stunned I couldn't find my voice.

When he huffed and got out of the car, I said, "I'll take you. How does four o'clock work?"

"Fine."

He shut the car door. I rolled the passenger-side window down and leaned over. "Should I pick you up here?"

"Fine."

He walked away up the rickety wooden steps that led to the front door. He didn't knock, but the door wasn't locked because he opened it and passed through.

I sat there until I finally had a clear enough head to drive to the Anderson's.

THE NEXT day, I parked my car and walked toward school. My thoughts were full of my Dad and our outing this afternoon. I was looking at the ground as I walked and didn't see Trina come out from behind the corner of the building.

I tensed when I saw her, but she went past me like she was a zombie. The circles under her eyes were so dark it looked as if she wore stage makeup. Her hair hung in limp, unwashed strands down her back. Even from a few yards away I could tell her clothes were crumpled and dirty.

There was a brief urge to reach out, to ask her what was wrong. She was my sister after all. But my survival was a greater urge. Trina was nothing but trouble and I kept that in the forefront of my mind as I hung back and let her pass into the school. She didn't lift her head once.

Maybe she knew Dad was going into hospice. Maybe she missed Mom and couldn't mask her sadness. Maybe she needed a fix and didn't have the money to pay for it.

I pushed Trina out of my mind and made it to class just before the bell rang.

IF SOMEONE completely awake and conscious could have an out-of-body experience then surely that's what I was having. There was no connection to my body as I drove my dad to a hospice center. Instead, I felt like I was floating somewhere high in the sky, right in the middle of a storm cloud heavy with promised downpours.

Dad gave me directions to the hospice in clipped, one syllable words. It was in the same town as Berkeley Mountain College. If I went to this school and if Dad was still…alive, I could visit him every day. Or as often as he would allow.

"Around that corner." He pointed with a finger that shook when he lifted it.

Soon we pulled up in front of a white, wooden building that looked like someone's home. "Is this it?"

He looked out the window. "Yeah. This is it." He pulled his gaze away and turned to me. With a sigh, he opened the door. "Thanks, Rowan."

As he got out of the car, a flash of fear shot through me. What if this was the last time I ever saw him? The thought sent terrified tremors through my body. It was strange. These past months with him gone and me living at the Anderson's, I hadn't missed him at all. But now, with the thought of never seeing him again, of him dying, I found I desperately wanted more time.

"Dad?"

He bent down and peered through the window.

"Call me, okay?"

He nodded.

"Dad?"

If there was a slither of irritation behind his gaze, it was gone in an instant. He almost seemed too tired to be irritated. I felt my heart start to crack.

"Can I come in with you? Look around?"

He nodded again. I put the car into *park* and got out. The sidewalk was empty except for an older man walking a white miniature poodle. They passed by and soon we were alone.

Dad held the door open for me, and we stepped into the small entrance side by side—just a daughter and her father. Though the tears didn't fall from my eyes they were inside of me, waiting for the dam to burst.

There was a small desk ahead where an older woman sat, her head bent over a notebook. I could see the patches of thinning brown hair on the top. "Can I help you?" she asked when she looked up.

"Jack Slone."

She nodded. I guess there was no need to ask if he was checking in. By merely looking at him, it was obvious that he was not going to live much longer.

"Your room is ready, but I need you to fill out some paperwork first. And who is this beautiful, young lady?"

Never one for personal questions, Dad threw suspicious eyes her way, but said anyway, "This is my daughter."

I forced a smile at the woman whose kind eyes told me she understood how difficult this moment was and that she'd witnessed it a hundred times over.

"You can have a seat by the fireplace. Let me know if you have any questions."

Dad didn't respond and turned to me. "You can go. Thanks for the ride."

"But…" I started to protest, however, the old Dad was back with his steely gaze, and I said, "Okay." I walked toward the door feeling like I was abandoning him.

"Dad?" I stopped.

He glanced up from the loveseat he'd sat on.

"Can I take you to lunch tomorrow?"

His iron expression didn't soften, but he did nod his head. "I'll be ready at noon."

I wanted to give him a smile, but I couldn't. The only thing I could do was stumble out of the building with smells of medicine and death chasing me. I would never forget how it felt to be with my dad at that moment, then leaving him behind in hospice care.

And as it turned out, it would be my last memory of him.

chapter fifteen

"WHAT DID you say?" My breath shot out of my mouth in short bursts as my chest heaved.

"Your father died overnight." Gran stood in the Anderson's doorway with Trina slumped on the small bench beside her. It was seven o'clock in the morning. "Rowan, honey, I'm so sorry."

"I just saw him yesterday," I said.

"Can we come in?" She glanced from me to Jess who was standing beside me.

When neither of us answered, she took a tentative step over the threshold. Wordless, Jess and I moved back and gave her room.

"Trina, come inside."

Without lifting her eyes, Trina pushed to her feet and walked into the house. Gran took off her coat then helped Trina out of hers. She did the same with the snow boots, helping Trina like she was a four-year-old girl again.

They stood in front of me, Gran waiting for some sort of direction or signal. Trina never moved her eyes from the floor, her blonde hair hanging in threads over her down-turned face.

Gran had aged years since last May. Her gray hair was short and choppy, standing in spikes all over her head. There was a stoop to her shoulders that had gotten worse since the last time I saw her. Her eyes were clear, but pained. She had known my dad since he was in high school even before he got Mom pregnant.

For several minutes the three of us didn't move, looking here, looking there. Before she rang the doorbell, I'd let Levi outside and he was still in the backyard. Delilah, though, jumped off the couch, shaking the floor when she landed and trotted over. She sniffed Gran's pants and Gran bent down to pet her head. She looked at Trina but lumbered over to me instead. I bent down and wrapped my arms around her solid body.

"Are the Andersons here?" Gran asked.

The house was as quiet as a deserted castle.

"No," Jess said. "They're at Mike's college."

Gran nodded. "I'll make you girls something to eat. I'm sure they won't mind." She passed by me without reaching out. Never one for idle hands, Gran went into the kitchen. Within a heartbeat she was back. "Trina, come with me."

Without a word, Trina followed. Soon the sound of pots banging against pans reverberated through the house.

I had wanted Gran to hug me. I wanted it so bad my heart fell to my knees when she simply walked past me. But I guess I'd created that—her keeping her distance. We hadn't spoken but five or ten times since May.

Today was different, though. Today I wanted someone who I knew loved me to pull me into their arms and tell me it would all be okay.

The room was starting to spin. Was there no one to comfort me? Mike. Gran. Mom. Trina. They all seemed so out of reach. A sob escaped my lips. I stumbled when I tried to move and someone caught me. It turned out there was someone to hug me—my best friend. She wrapped her long, thin arms around me and held me tight while I sobbed into her flannel pajamas.

SOMETIME LATER, with the nauseating remnant of eggs wafting through the house, I sat in the chair in front of the fireplace.

Jess was in the kitchen with Gran. Trina had been escorted up to my bedroom to lie down after she had started wailing in the middle of eating her cereal. Gran must've given her a sedative or something because it was disturbingly quiet upstairs.

"You're taking care of the arrangements?" Jess was asking Gran.

I stared into the black pit that had been alive with fire a few days ago when Mike's friends were over, when Mike was home, when my dad was still alive.

No. No. No. He'd only just come back. He seemed changed. Sorry for the past. He seemed like he might want a relationship with me. *No!* Grief tore through me, ripping through my insides. *No!* I rocked back and forth, clutching my stomach as that simple, yet devastating word rang through my head.

At some point, Jess sat down on the floor in front of me. She started to pick tiny threads out of the carpet, and I watched her do it. Levi trotted over and sat on his haunches by my side, his head on the armrest.

Delilah made her way over and sat by my other side, letting out a long moan as she did so. The sweetness of their faces with their large, searching eyes, and Jess' closeness, was the only silver lining in an otherwise very black morning.

JESS CALLED Miss J. to tell her what happened. Gran had been on the phone most of the morning making arrangements. She didn't ask for my help or input, but I could hear every word she said from where I was sitting. Levi had managed to jump onto my lap. His weight and his size almost smothered me, but I was thankful for his closeness.

"Call Janie, please," I asked Jess at one point. "She just promoted me to assistant manager."

"I did. She said to call her if you need anything. I really like her." Jess was eating a bowl of cereal as Delilah watched her with unveiled envy. "You need to eat."

I shook my head. Time eased back into a mindless void. Gran darted in and out of the room. She never spoke to me. At one point, she did put her hand on my shoulder. It was a hollow touch, though. What I wanted, and needed, was for her to pull me to her and hold me the way she did the night my dad beat me up.

Trina had stayed upstairs most of the day, and I'd forgotten about her until she came flying down the stairs midafternoon, raced out the front door, and let it slam shut behind her.

"What was that about?" Jess demanded.

I shrugged and looked out the window. Trina was leaning in the passenger-side window of a car I didn't recognize. Within minutes, she was back in the house and up the stairs.

"She's on drugs," I told Jess.

"Doesn't surprise me, the little tramp."

Gran's voice droned on from the kitchen, something about flower type, arrangements, and cost. More time passed. Gazing into the empty fireplace hadn't changed a thing. My mom was still in jail. My sister was still messed up. And my dad was still dead.

HOURS LATER, I was in the kitchen arguing with Jess about food.

"Rowan?" Mrs. Anderson's voice rang through the house. "Rowan, where are you?"

I walked down the hall from the kitchen.

"Oh, my sweet child." She folded me into her arms, enveloping me in her perfumed softness.

Mr. Anderson came up behind her and placed a hand on my shoulder. "I'm so sorry for your loss, Rowan."

"Thank you." My words were muffled by Mrs. Anderson's scarf.

"Rowan?"

I pulled back at the sound of *that* voice. Mike stood in the living room, too, all tall and handsome and the answer to so many of my prayers. As I stumbled toward him, he opened his arms and caught me, like he always did, like I knew he would.

"I'm so sorry, Rowan."

My arms wrapped around his solid body, pulling him toward me, trying to absorb the feel of him. "I didn't know you were coming."

"How could I *not* come? I want to be here for you."

"Hi, Jess," Mrs. Anderson said and gave her a hug. "I'm so glad you've been here for Rowan."

Jess nodded and slipped out of Mrs. Anderson's embrace. She sat on the couch and pet Levi's dark head.

"How long are you in town for?" I asked Mike, still clutching him.

"I can stay until tomorrow afternoon. I'll leave right after the funeral."

The funeral. Even seeing Mike couldn't diminish the gray cloud that hung over everything. He was home because my dad had died. He was alive a few days ago. Now he was dead. And we were having a funeral.

"We haven't eaten dinner yet," Mrs. Anderson said. "I'll go make something, and you can let me know what I can do to help."

She hurried out of the room and Mr. Anderson followed her. Gran and Trina had left about an hour ago. If Gran noticed that the sullen Trina was gone and had been replaced by an overly chipper and bouncy Trina, she didn't say. To Trina's credit, she did manage to hide it pretty well.

WHEN MIKE came into my room that night, he held me in his arms for a long, long time, running his fingers through my hair, up and down my back, over my arm. It wasn't a time for more than that. Not now.

Sleep did not come easily and I lay awake for hours, long after Mike's hand had stilled and his breathing deepened into soft snores. But at some point, I fell into the welcome abyss.

I jolted awake after only an hour with a desperate need to feel Mike's closeness. He was leaving today, and I didn't know when I'd feel him near me again.

I touched his neck, his lips, ran a hand over his chest until he awoke, too. He turned to me as I turned to him. Our clothes flew to a pile on the floor.

We had been together too many times to count, but this was different in so many ways; not the least of which we had never been skin-to-skin before because I never took off my shirt. But tonight, or this morning, or whatever time it was, there was such a need in me I couldn't resist and I'd let him take off my shirt. It was dark, so dark I couldn't even see his face.

For the first time ever I didn't think of my scars. I just thought of Mike and let his closeness obliterate everything else.

AFTERWARD, HE held me so close I couldn't tell where his bare skin ended and mine began. Even though it was cold outside, it was warm in my bed and I could feel the sweat on his skin.

"I love you, Rowan."

"I love you, too." I snuggled close to him and for the first time in days, my heart was happy. I closed my eyes and drifted off into a dreamless place where I was content and nothing could invade to take that away. That was until the faint glow of sunrise came creeping into the room and Mike saw my arm when I moved in my sleep.

"What the hell? Rowan, what's on your arm?" He had a hold of my wrist and was lifting my arm in the air before I was even fully awake.

I yanked away from him and jumped to my feet. With one hasty motion, I pulled a sweater over my head. The dark, gray light was just enough to show Mike's expression, and it was a mixture of horror and disbelief.

"Are you okay?" he demanded. "What is that?"

I forced a laugh that in no way fooled him or me. "I'm fine. It's nothing."

"Are you sick? Let me see." He scrambled to his feet.

"No!" I stepped away from him.

"Did you do that to yourself?" I could see the truth wash over his face like an icy rain. "Did you?" He reached a hand toward me, but I took another step back.

"Look. It's no big deal. It's just something I used to do. Let's not make a federal case of it."

"Not make a case of it? You used to cut yourself, didn't you? I've heard of girls doing that, I just never thought it would be my girlfriend!"

"You should go. I need to get ready for my dad's funeral."

"I'm not leaving until you talk to me."

"That's not true. You're leaving in a few hours, right? Going back to school as soon as the funeral is over?"

"That's not fair, Rowan. I have to get back for practice."

"When is your next practice? When is your next game?" I paused then asked, "Why do you have to rush back?"

His eyes narrowed. "I just do. I have to get back. I have classes. Workouts. And yes, there is practice. We need to keep in shape over the winter."

It was light enough now in the room that he could see my eyes roll.

"What was that for? You don't believe me?"

"Look. I appreciate you coming home for my dad's funeral, but I need you more than that, more than in just a crisis." And that was it. Mike was amazing when I really needed him. Where he was lacking was being the everyday boyfriend, mostly because he wasn't even around and didn't seem to be making much of an effort to change that.

"What is that supposed to mean?"

"It means that I want to see you more often and actually feel like you *want* to be around me."

"But I do! What are you talking about?"

This pinball of a conversation was sucking the life out of me. "I have to get ready. I don't want to be late for a funeral. Or did you forget this day is about my dad and not about me?"

"I haven't forgotten. But Rowan, this is your dad's funeral. You haven't exactly been close to him. We need to talk about *you*."

"We don't need to talk about me. How could you be so heartless?" My voice rose with each word.

"We've got to get you help. You can't go on like this."

"I'm not your charity case. I'm not someone you need to fix!"

"But you're sick, Rowan. Sick."

"I am not sick!" My screams echoed through the room. I heard a door close out in the hall, but it didn't stop me. "I'm not sick, and I don't need your help." My breath came in quick bursts and my heart pounded like someone was taking a hammer to it. "I'm fine," I seethed through clenched teeth.

"You are not fine. Your arm looks like a carving block." He grabbed my wrist, and I wasn't strong enough to wrench free. Then he yanked up the sleeve of my sweater. His grasp hurt, digging into my flesh. "Look at this! How can you say you're fine?"

This was the worst moment of my life—my shame out there for him to see in the now sunlit room. The light caught the scars perfectly.

As he stared at me, I could feel judgment creep into his mind, like dark, poisonous tentacles covering his brain and altering it; altering the way he would forever look at me.

His grasp eased and I wrenched away, jumping from him. "Don't ever grab me like that again."

His jaw clenched and his pine-colored eyes flashed with anger.

"Get out of here. I need to get ready. If you don't want to honor my father, then don't bother coming to the funeral."

This time it was hurt that flashed behind his eyes and it tugged at my heart; but I couldn't forget the accusation, the declaration of my sickness. He turned and walked away without another word, slamming the door on his way out.

TEARS COVERED my face. I walked to the window and looked out. Then I used all my strength to shove the window open. It was early still and the sun cast pink rays along the horizon. Wind blew through the bare tree limbs, not like a storm was coming but like the angels were restless, wanting. I leaned out the window to feel the unrest.

I knelt down and rested my chin on the sill. With slow movements, I lifted my arm, casting the inside of it out toward the sun. It didn't shrivel up and die. It didn't yank its brightness away from me in disdain.

I looked down at my arm, from the area above my elbow to just below, that was covered with more red skin than white. I started to count the marks:

One.
Two.
Three.
Four.
Five.
Six...

And there in the midst of all the angry red slashes, the blaring red *A* I'd carved into my skin in the bathroom of the hospital; the day my life had been redefined from the killer of my brother to the daughter of a murderer.

The sun was higher now. I closed my eyes and lifted my face toward it. The air was so cold my fingers were turning numb. I stayed there for several minutes until I finally pushed to my feet and got ready for my father's funeral.

chapter sixteen

DAD WAS not a religious man so his funeral was held at the funeral home, an old, paint-chipped building that had been a part of this town long before I was born. Mrs. Anderson asked her preacher to conduct the service. I guess, since I'd been going to church there for the past several months, he was my preacher, too. I found little solace, though, in his tall, overly thin frame, slightly crooked at the shoulder like he was always bending to the side.

He was standing at the front of a small, square room when we arrived, leaning toward the casket as if he were standing guard, or offering tickets for the next show. He wore his most solemn expression, like it was frozen on his face and had been there when he woke up this morning. Had he practiced different expressions in the mirror? Did preachers do that?

The casket was just to his right, almost like it was floating in midair. The top half was open, and I could see just a hint of the body inside. If I didn't look directly at it, there was no confirmation that it was my dad lying there. It was someone else.

When the preacher moved toward me, my eyes betrayed me, moving to the casket. Suddenly, the one thing I couldn't look at directly was the only thing I could see.

The casket was made of shiny, dark brown wood with gold handles that gleamed too bright in the dreary room. A small bouquet of flowers lay across the bottom half of the casket where Dad's hips lay under the closed section. I wondered if they were Gran's touch.

The preacher made it to my side, but I didn't look at him. There was nothing else but the casket with Dad's ashen face and folded hands, and the severe ache of my heart. An earthquake started in my toes and erupted through my body until I was shaking all over like I was stuck in the eye of a storm.

"I can't go in there." I clutched Jess' arm.

"Rowan, take your time." Mrs. Anderson caressed my cheek. "Take your time."

Jess put her arms around me and her warmth fought to settle me. It didn't work.

"Oh my God. Oh my God." I didn't cry, but I couldn't stop repeating this phrase over and over to myself until Miss J. leaned down into my face.

"Rowan!" Her voice cracked like a whip and the words stopped in my throat. "It's okay. You're going to be okay." She put her hands on my shoulders and squeezed.

I nodded, feeling so unattached from this moment that I didn't feel my feet carry me forward.

"Rowan, hello." The preacher held out his hand, but I didn't take it. Instead, I stepped around him and walked to the casket.

Dad's face was angry even in death. No matter how hard the funeral director tried, he couldn't mask the resentment and anger that shaped Jack Slone.

He almost looked like the man I remembered. Or rather, he looked like a wax copy. His lips were pale, almost white. A fake color was swiped across his cheeks, but it made them too pink, too clownish.

I resisted the urge to reach out and poke him, thinking somewhere deep in my brain that that was a kid thing to do. And I wasn't a kid anymore, no matter how lost I felt at that moment.

Then arms were around me. I didn't know whose they were, only that they weren't Mike's. He should be the one holding me, shouldn't he? I looked to my side and realized it was Gran, dressed head-to-toe in black. Even the circles under her eyes were black.

She didn't say anything. Trina joined us and Gran put an arm around her, too. The three of us stared down at my dead father lying in the dead wood casket. My heart was breaking. What made it worse was that I didn't fully understand why.

We were not close as father and daughter. In fact, for most of my life, I felt like Dad hated me. We didn't toss the baseball, or practice the waltz, or go to get ice cream when I brought home a good report card. We didn't do any of those things. He stalked around the house like a simmering pot of boiling water, and I cowered around the house like a little mouse terrified of drawing too much attention to myself.

But I could feel it—my heart breaking, almost like it was a dried piece of clay that was crumbling in my hands. I was surprised and devastated all at once. Why had it taken his death to realize I loved him?

"Shall we get started?" The preacher's voice made me want to cover my ears with my hands.

Gran led me and Trina to the front row. I sat on the aisle seat with Gran beside me and Trina beside her. Dad's casket was only a few feet from me. If I reached out, I wouldn't be able to touch him, but his face was so close I could see the pasty-white makeup.

As the preacher greeted everyone in a low, droning voice, I watched my father's chest, waiting for it to rise and fall. At one point I thought it did, and I shuddered, grabbing Gran's hand. When she squeezed her bony fingers around mine, I realized I was mistaken and sat back in my seat.

Throughout the service Gran kept my hand in hers, but I couldn't feel anything. I only knew it was there because I stared down at our hands and saw that the fingers were intertwined. She was also holding Trina's hand.

I turned in my seat to see who was there. There were eleven people: me, Trina, Gran, Jess, Mike, Mrs. Anderson, Mr. Anderson, Miss J., Janie, Angel, and Dad's friend, Ron.

The preacher asked if anyone wanted to say anything, but no one spoke up. What was there to say? After an uncomfortable silence, the preacher cleared his throat and asked us to bow our heads. Within the blink of an eye the service was over, and people were passing me between them like I was an infant at a baptism. How ironic that the hugs I had longed for yesterday only made me feel sick today. Even Gran's arms made my insides cringe.

A statue couldn't have stood more still than me, though, with stony hands folded across my stomach. People's words and caresses rolled off me like rain droplets. And far too soon after, I found myself in a car, driving to the cemetery.

I was in the car with Miss J. and Jess. Mike and his parents were in the car behind us, then Gran and Trina. Janie and Angel had hugged me tight at the end of the ceremony and quietly slipped away. The rest of us followed a long black hearse that meandered through our small country town.

This area had one place where most people were buried. I had never been there and as we passed underneath the iron arch that marked the entrance, I knew I never wanted to come back. It was a dismal place filled with fake flowers and wasted lives.

The hearse drove past row after row of stone tombstones standing stoic like small soldiers. A light, freezing rain blanketed the surrounding trees with tiny crystals. When the car stopped near the burial site, I got out and felt the rain cascade over me like a caress from death itself.

Ahead, there was a canopy. Under that canopy there was a hole. And in that hole was where my dad would rest.

My heels sunk into the earth as I walked arm in arm with Jess to the burial site. Since Dad had few friends, Mrs. Anderson asked men from church to carry the casket. These men spilled out of the hearse and then proceeded to pull my father's casket out of the back.

Their feet squished into the sodden earth, and I could tell they struggled to keep the heavy wood on their shoulders. But they made it and rested the casket on the top of some sort of metal frame.

After the men were free of the weight, they moved to the back of our miniscule group. I wished I could stand back there with them, aloof and untouched by what was happening. But I couldn't. I was here, seated once again in front of my dad, my heart hurting so bad I feared it would burst. Then they could bury me with him when I died.

The preacher started to speak. I would hear his somber cadence in my nightmares if I let myself listen. His voice quivered in the cold. I could see his breath escape his mouth, like little ghosts, each time he spoke. But I didn't hear the words. I heard nothing.

Then everyone was standing. Hands were back on my shoulders. Somehow Trina's hand had made it into mine. Jess stood on my other side and my ears reopened.

The preacher was still talking. "The Andersons have been nice enough to invite everyone back to their house for a light lunch. You are all welcome."

Mike stood behind me and put an arm around my shoulders. "I'm so sorry, Rowan. I know you two didn't always get along, but I'm sure it still hurts."

I nodded. His arm felt heavy, weighing me down when all I really wanted to do was fly away—fly far, far away. I let him comfort me because I knew that was the right thing to do.

When Gran came up, he squeezed my shoulder and moved away. Gran was crying, tears pooling in her deep-set wrinkles. "I've known him since he was in high school. I just can't believe it. Despite everything he did, he was like a son to me." She covered her mouth with a tissue and sobbed into it. She shook her head and walked over to the casket where she pulled a rose from the arrangement and tucked it into her purse.

"You okay?" Trina asked. Her hand slid into mine.

I nodded. "You?"

"Yeah, I guess. I mean, it doesn't feel real. It doesn't feel like he's really in there. Ya know?"

I did know.

"I'm going to go see Mom later. Gran's coming, too. Do you want to come?"

I shook my head.

For once, Trina didn't make a nasty comment. Instead she said, "I'm going to walk Gran back to the car. See you at the Anderson's."

I nodded again and watched her walk toward Gran, her heels sinking into the earth. That was the most normal conversation Trina and I had had in years.

Miss J. and Jess flanked either side of me like two stoic bodyguards. I didn't try to smile—they wouldn't expect it anyway. "I need a minute, okay?" I said. "I'll be right there."

"Okay," Miss J. said. She and Jess took several steps away, opened an umbrella, and stood under it with the preacher. They were just out of earshot, which was good, because I had something to say.

I fell to my knees by his casket, my weight pushing into the soft earth.

"You're a bastard," I whispered. I laid my hands on the smooth wood, watching my fingers shake from the cold, from his death. "You were a bully and a bad father." Tears started in my eyes. "But you were *my* father, and I can't believe you're actually in there."

The moisture blinded me. "You don't belong in there." I shook my head, my hair swinging around my face. It was as if the more I believed he shouldn't be in there, the more everything would change and he would suddenly come walking up the road.

"I didn't kill Aidan. You know that now. After all of these years, you know that. I didn't kill him. He was a light. I loved him so much. I. Didn't. Kill. Him."

Sobs wracked through my body, leaving my shoulders heaving.

"But I did love you." I took several deep, shuddering breaths. "Somewhere inside my heart, I still love you. And I'm sorry that you're gone. And you know what, Dad?" I laid my forehead against the wood. "I know you loved me, too."

Then I collapsed and stayed there until Miss J. and Jess picked me up and carried me away.

WHEN I left Dad's side something in me felt different, like I was floating through the air, suspended in time and space. The freezing rain had changed to snow and soon the air in front of me was alight with white, miniscule angels.

"It's beautiful." I stopped. The burial site was to my back, the car parked ahead. But right here in front of me now was a parade of hundreds of fluffy little bursts of beauty.

The sky was a grayish blue, cloud-covered but still bright somehow. Even the clouds couldn't stop the sun shining. But it was the snowflakes that were mesmerizing. As they landed on my face, cooling my skin, I raised my palms. Then I closed my eyes and relished the feel of the flakes against my lids. It was almost like little angels were planting light kisses on my skin.

When I finally opened my eyes again, I saw that Miss J. and Jess were doing the same thing. And on that day of all days, when death had entered my life for the second time in my eighteen years, I felt okay.

"I'm ready."

chapter seventeen

WHEN THE three of us got to the Anderson's, Mrs. Anderson and Gran were in the kitchen laying out food. Mike and Trina sat in the living room. Mike was on the couch surrounded by Delilah and Levi, Trina on the opposite chair. She was flung back in the seat, arms hanging over the armrests, like she was as bored as life could make her. But when she saw us, she popped up, dashed across the room, and flung herself into me. I stumbled backward and Miss J. helped keep me from falling. Though Trina clung to me like a lifeline, my arms stayed by my sides.

"Oh, Rowan! Thank God you're here. I need my sister!" Suddenly she was weeping into my shoulder. "I can't believe he's gone," She sniffed. "I just can't believe it."

Trina's wailing brought in Gran and Mrs. Anderson from the kitchen and Mr. Anderson from the study.

"Is everything okay?" Mike's dad asked, his voice gruff.

Mrs. Anderson, though, always ready to lend a warm embrace, hurried over. "Dear sweet girls. It's okay. It'll be okay."

I bristled at Mrs. Anderson calling Trina a *dear sweet girl*. But I didn't want to lose that feeling of contentment I'd gained at the cemetery. If ignoring Trina's neurotic rants accomplished that, then I would leave her be.

Mike's eyes locked on mine and after Mrs. Anderson peeled a heaving Trina off my body, I went to sit beside him on the couch. Several inches separated us.

"How are you holding up?" he asked, stroking Delilah's head. The dog opened one eye and snorted. Levi, all eighty pounds of him, tried to sit on my lap again. Most of him fit, pushing me deep into the couch's soft cushions. I leaned back so I could look at Mike.

"I'm good, all things considered."

"It was a nice service."

I nodded. "Yes. It was nice."

Several minutes passed, each of us petting our own dog, neither of us speaking. Finally, he said, "I have to leave in an hour. Can we go somewhere and talk?"

Leaving in an hour. It was almost like he hadn't even been here. But he had been. And he'd seen the scars to prove it.

"Do you want to go upstairs?"

He shook his head. "Dad's in the kitchen so we can go into the study."

I nodded and gave Levi a gentle push until he moved off my lap. When Mike slid out from under Delilah, she tilted her head up then turned her butt toward him.

"Where are you two going?" Gran asked, though her words were curious, not invasive.

"We're going to go talk a minute before he goes."

"Okay." She smiled—not the wide kind, but the soft, sweet grandma kind. I didn't return the smile. Something told me that what was coming didn't call for cheery expressions.

MR. ANDERSON'S study was small and square, an addition to the original house with red brick walls and drafty windows. There was a fireplace across from the wooden desk and several diplomas and artwork leaned against one wall, waiting to be hung. A brown leather recliner sat in one corner and that was the only furniture other than the desk and chair.

I liked this room, but I rarely came in here even though Mr. Anderson told me I could use the computer anytime. I didn't belong in the middle of Mr. Anderson's bills, letters, and magazines. Besides, I had my own computer, an ancient laptop that ran slower than a turtle racing against a hare. But it was mine and worked well enough.

Mike shut the door and turned. "Are you okay?"

I rubbed my arms. "I'm hanging in there."

"You're not going to, you know." He looked at my arm and waved his hand at me. "Cut yourself."

My mouth fell open. When I searched his face, I found concern there, but I also found judgment. "No, Mike. I'm not. I haven't done that in months, and I don't plan to start doing it now."

"Don't plan to? You're sick, Rowan. Sick. I mean, you need help."

Fury erupted in me like a volcano. "Listen." I stepped forward. "I don't need your judgment or your accusations or your false worry. I'm fine. I can take care of myself."

"It doesn't seem like it to me."

My hand itched to swing out and slap his handsome face. But that face wasn't as handsome as it used to be. It was harder, more angular, more severe. He'd shaved this morning, but dark stubble still peeped through. Something had changed in my boyfriend since he left this summer; something that I did not like.

Maybe, though, just maybe, I had changed, too.

"I've said it before, and I'll say it again—I am not your charity case. Back off, Mike. This is in the past."

"But how? How is it in the past?" He stared at me a hard moment then blurted, "That's why you always wear long sleeves. My God, Rowan, you can't even wear normal clothes."

If someone threw me into the middle of a tornado, I wouldn't have felt more frazzled, confused, stirred up. "This is me, Mike.

Take it or leave it." The shakiness in my voice disproved my strong words.

He was silent, eyes focused on my arm. It started to burn under his gaze, and I had to clench my fist to keep from scratching the dozen lines, from tracing the ugly *A*.

Sometimes I still wanted to cut but I didn't.

I. Didn't. Cut.

My legs were covered in silky light hairs because I refused to hold a razor between my fingers. I'd bent over backward, writing in my journal, studying late into the night, putting more hours in at the shelter, just to occupy my mind.

I didn't cut anymore.

I didn't cut anymore.

I don't cut anymore.

I don't cut anymore.

"I DON'T CUT anymore!" A soft knock on the door was the only thing that interrupted my screams.

"Rowan, are you okay?" Miss J.'s soft voice carried through the heavy wood.

My body erupted in shivers and shakes, and soon I had to sit in that large leather chair, the first time my butt had ever been on its surface.

I locked eyes with Mike, willing him to expose my secret, willing him to expose his judgment of it. But he looked away, unable to hold my gaze.

"We'll be right out," I said.

"Okay. Let me know if you need anything."

We were quiet as the ticking of Mr. Anderson's clock drummed on.

"I need to go," Mike said. "I have practice tomorrow morning."

I nodded, a welcome numbness washing over me.

He didn't move, though. I stared into the fireplace, unable to look at this stranger standing before me.

"Rowan, I love you."

I couldn't tame the flash of anger in my eyes. "You have a funny way of showing it," I spat.

"No, I don't," he spat back. "If I didn't love you, I wouldn't care what you did to yourself."

My teeth clenched so hard, I thought I heard them crack. "If you love me, then you have to understand that *that* part of my life is over. I don't…do that anymore."

"I wish I could believe you."

"Then why don't you? I've never lied to you."

"No, but you sure have kept a lot from me. I thought we were closer than that."

His words were like jabs from a sharp knife, piercing straight to my soul.

"No one knew. No one knows. Mike, this has nothing to do with you."

"It has everything to do with me. I'm your boyfriend. We're supposed to be close, or had you forgotten that little detail?"

I wanted to pick up the silver cup that Mr. Anderson won at a golf tournament and hurl it at his head. Never had I felt like being so violent toward him, but there was no reasoning here. Some of what he said made sense, but fury clouded over everything that came out of my mouth. He knew my secret and he was using it against me; using it to *judge* me.

Several words danced across my tongue and every single one was shaped with a fanged bite, shaped to hurt him as much as the accusation behind his eyes was hurting me. But something stopped me. Instead, I swallowed those shredding words and said, "It's time for you to go, isn't it? You don't want to be late."

He tilted his head to the side and narrowed his eyes. I couldn't stand another minute of his brain working to define me, to define me because I used to cut.

I jumped out of the chair. "I need to walk Levi." I swept out the door without so much as a whispered word or a gentle touch of goodbye.

All heads turned toward me when I breezed into the living room like I didn't have a care in the world. "I'm going to go for a walk. I'll be back." Levi must've known something was up because he was already at the door, standing underneath his leash.

"I'm coming with you," said Miss J. It wasn't a question. It was a statement, and I didn't argue.

Miss J. put on her coat. Jess was asleep on the couch, her hand resting on the tiny little mound of her stomach.

WE WERE ten minutes into the walk before Miss J. spoke. "Is there anything you want to talk about?" We were at the edge of the park near Mike's house. For a place that was usually crowded with people and animals there was no one else around. I unleashed Levi, threw his ball, and watched him tear off after it. I sat on a bench. Miss. J. sat beside me.

"What's going on?" she asked again, though her words weren't demanding or invasive. Care shaped her words, and I welcomed that. But instead of answering her, I shimmied out of my coat and pulled up the sleeve on my left arm.

Miss J. gasped, but then I watched her lips clamp shut as she reached out her hand and ran feather-light fingers over the scars. "Do they still hurt?"

"No. They're healed."

"When was the last time...?"

"That day at the hospital. Last year."

"When you found out the truth?"

"Yeah."

"And you haven't since?"

"No."

She turned in her seat so she could better see my arm and pulled it close to her eyes. "I can guess what the *A* stands for?"

I nodded. Levi didn't bring his ball back. As was typical of him, he seemed to sense that I needed a moment.

She pulled my sleeve down and sat back, scanning the horizon.

"That's it?" I watched her from the corner of my eye.

"That's it." She didn't turn back toward me. "I worry about you, Rowan. But I am also excited for you. There are great things waiting for you." She patted my leg. "You're going to be okay. I can feel it."

We sat there for a long time watching a pair of hawks that nested nearby, their huge bodies burdening the thin branches of the tree.

"You showing me this. Does this have something to do with the fight you and Mike just had?"

I nodded. "He didn't know. And he found out. He started calling me sick, telling me there's something wrong with me."

"I see."

"Yeah." Words like *asshole* and *jerk* came to mind, but I didn't say them.

"And where do things stand now?"

I shrugged. "Who knows?"

Minute after minute passed by and my nose started to run. Was Dad somewhere up above looking down on this holy mess? Would he be surprised to know what I'd done to myself? Back at the gas station, he'd said that he could tell I'd moved on. It was laughable, although it wasn't, how little he'd known about me.

There was a pain inside my chest, inside my body, touching every part my blood touched. I tried to pull back the good feelings I'd had at the cemetery, the feelings of optimism, hope. Every few thoughts I felt a slither of those feelings, but right now they were out of reach.

Miss J. scratched the arm of my jacket with her finger. "Do you want to go back?"

"We probably should." I was unable to bear the thought that I could go back to the house on the day of my father's funeral, and not see Mike before he left, even though I was furious with him. "Levi, come."

Levi bounded over, and I clicked the leash to his collar. We walked back to the Anderson's in silence. When we went inside, Jess was awake and eating from a huge plate of food. Trina sat nearby, watching her eat, a look of disgust on her face. I could hear Gran, and Mr. and Mrs. Anderson talking in the kitchen. If Mike was in there, I didn't hear his voice. He was probably upstairs packing, eager to get away as fast as he could.

I sat beside Jess and pulled a carrot off her plate. "How was your nap?"

She forced a laugh. "It was good. Much needed. My second one of the day. Now I'm starving."

"Obviously."

This time her laugh came easier. But Trina noticed. She looked at Jess' food, and I could see the wheels turning in her blonde head.

"You're pregnant, aren't you?" Trina blurted.

"Go to hell, twerp," Jess said.

"Oh my God, you are so pregnant." Trina started to laugh, a high cackling sound that made my eardrums hurt.

"Trina, don't be a bitch. You don't know what you're talking about," I said, stealing a glance at Miss J.

She was watching us closely.

"I *do* know what I'm talking about. Remember?"

How could we forget? Getting knocked up by a black kid my dad would never approve of, blaming it on Mike, then losing the baby the day she tried to kill herself. No, there was no way to forget all that.

"Trina, leave. You're not wanted here," I said.

"I can be anywhere I want. And I want to be right here, watching Jess feed her face and her unborn baby." She laughed again, an ugly, scratchy sound. "Is it that old guy's? You know, our old substitute teacher?" She snapped her fingers and looked at the ceiling. "What was his name? He was gone by the time I got to high school, but I think he substituted for the middle school, too. Peter…? Patrick…?" She fidgeted in her seat. "Paul! That's it!"

She shoved a finger at Jess. Laughter rang throughout the room. "You are so pregnant by that old man."

"Out!" Miss J. jumped to her feet and pointed at the front door.

Trina snarled her lip. "What? I didn't do anything. She's the one who's knocked up." Her laughter trilled up to the ceiling and back down to the floor. I winced and fought the urge to cover my ears.

"Trina, I said *out*. Either listen or I'll call your grandmother in here and see what she has to say."

Jess covered her face with her hand, the food forgotten on her lap.

Trina didn't head outside. Instead, she stood to her feet, flashed a smirk at Jess, and walked toward the kitchen.

"I'm sorry. I shouldn't have spoken to her like that." Miss J. shook her head as if she was clearing out the cobwebs.

"Don't apologize. She's a bitch," I said.

Jess stayed quiet. She stared at the books on the coffee table, but I doubted she'd be able to tell me a single title if I asked.

"Jess?" Miss J. asked. "Is it true? Are you pregnant?"

Jess didn't respond, like she didn't hear her. Miss J. looked at me and with the slightest motion, I nodded. Miss J. fell back against the couch, closed her eyes, and her lips started to move. I think she was praying.

chapter eighteen

MIKE DUMPED his bag in the front hall. "I need to get on the road."

"Oh, honey." Mrs. Anderson went to him. "Be careful and call me when you get there to let me know you made it."

He kissed her cheek.

"Bye, son," Mr. Anderson said, giving him a hug.

"Have a safe trip," Gran called as she walked into the living room.

"Bye, Mike," Trina sing-songed, back in the chair, twirling a long blonde strand of hair between her fingers.

"Rowan?" He turned to me.

"I'll walk you out."

I pulled on my coat and boots then followed him outside. The blast of air was frigid, but not nearly as cold as the vibes bouncing between us. He threw his bag into the back of his car and turned. "I don't know what to say. You need help."

I sliced a hand through the air. "Don't."

His eyes narrowed. Finally, he shrugged. "Okay. Then, I guess that's it."

I wrapped my arms around my chest, trying to prevent the chill that was settling into my bones. "I guess it is."

"I'll call you."

I'll call you? That was it? Really and truly *it*? I wished for the numbness of earlier to wash over me again. "Fine. Whatever."

"Okay. Well, bye." He paused and I didn't think he was going to reach out to me, but he did and kissed my cheek. My skin was so cold I barely felt it.

"Bye," I choked as he pulled back.

He got into his car and backed out of the driveway. Something had changed between us. It was as simple, as easy, and as devastating as that.

THE BENCH was cold beneath me, but I didn't notice. The only thing I was conscious of was that the space in the driveway was empty again. Mike's car was gone, leaving a big, gaping hole where his Mazda should be.

If noxious, poisonous gas started rising out of that black space, I wouldn't have been surprised and I would have inhaled it willingly. Maybe it would've stopped my heart before it could turn into a cracked, irreparable, frozen mass.

Snow started to fall around me—large, fluffy flakes like tufts of cotton being dumped from the sky. I held my hand out beyond the reach of the porch and let them fall onto my skin. They melted into tiny, miniscule puddles.

When the front door opened, my palm was covered in water.

"Thank you for having us over." Gran walked onto the porch.

"You are welcome here anytime." Mrs. Anderson hugged Gran and Mr. Anderson shook her hand.

"Trina, it was good to see you again." Mrs. Anderson hugged Trina. "Stop by and see me if you want to talk."

Talk about what?

Gran stopped in front of me. "There are some things that I need to give you, things of your father's. Come over tonight or tomorrow. If not right away, then soon." She rubbed my arm. "You'll want these things." The skin around her eyes crinkled as she forced a sympathetic smile.

I nodded and let her hug me.

Trina breezed past me. I thought she was going to ignore me, but she turned suddenly, grabbed my arms, and planted a sloppy, wet kiss on my cheek. "I love you, Rowan! I miss you so much. Please come home. I want my sister back." With the flip of a switch the tears started down her face, creating little pale rivers down her freshly applied makeup. She dropped her arms and darted toward Gran's car. Just before she ducked inside, Trina turned and flashed a smirk that was gone so fast, I wasn't sure anyone saw but me.

"ROWAN? ARE you okay?" Mrs. Anderson moved to my side by the window. Mike had been gone about an hour and the hollowness in my heart was only expanding. I missed him.

"I'm fine." I stared at the emptiness on the driveway.

"Did something happen with Mike?"

I shook my head. The black pavement started to swirl under my unblinking gaze.

"Do you want to talk about it?" She rubbed a light path between my shoulders, but I barely felt it.

"No," I whispered. "Not today."

"Okay. I understand." She planted a kiss on my head and gave me a hug. It felt warm, secure, and safe. But there was something else bothering me, something besides Mike that had entirely to do with his mom. "What did you mean when you told Trina she could come and talk to you?"

She sighed. "She's suffering, Rowan. She needs guidance."

"Guidance? For what?" A guide to lead her straight to Hell? I doubted she needed help with that.

"She's lost and probably always has been. I think what happened last year has had a great impact on her. I know she misses you terribly, and your mom."

"How do you know all of this?"

She watched the snowflakes melt into the grass. "She started going to the youth group at church on Wednesday nights."

"Trina is going to church? *Your* church?"

"Trina started going to the youth group at the beginning of the school year. She really seems to like it. She would come to Sunday service if she didn't think it would bother you."

Maybe the cold had frozen my ears, and I wasn't hearing her correctly. Trina had been a part of Mrs. Anderson's life, and I didn't know anything about it? Why would Mrs. Anderson allow that?

Mrs. Anderson would never do anything to hurt me. I knew she loved me almost like her own child. But wouldn't she think that this would hurt me? Was I no consideration in Mrs. Anderson's moral obligation to save every lost kid out there?

"One day it would be nice if you went on Wednesdays, too. Maybe the two of you can go together. Start to repair what's been damaged."

Shock and revulsion swallowed my words.

"Blood is thicker than water, right? Isn't that how the saying goes? And we know that God encourages forgiveness. Maybe it's time to forgive."

I turned to her. "And forgive my mom, too?"

"At some point, Rowan, you have to move on. Forgive, if not forget."

"And you think that forgiveness should extend to not only my lying sister, who accused Mike of rape and getting her pregnant, but also to my mother who killed my brother and let me take the blame for seven years?"

She let out a heavy, weighted breath. "Perhaps now isn't the time to talk about this. Come away from the window. Let me make you some tea. It's been such a long day. I'll have Mr. Anderson make a fire, and we can sit around and watch bad TV all night. Why don't you have Jess spend the night? I know how close you two are and she's always welcome here." Words tumbled out of her mouth in a long breath of hot air.

I let Mrs. Anderson lead me away from the window. I fell down beside Jess with Levi between my feet and Miss J. soon by my other side.

"Is everything okay?" Miss J. whispered.

I shook my head. Two pairs of eyes were on me—Miss J.'s brown ones and Jess' blue ones.

But I couldn't speak. Someone had grasped my brain and shook it so hard that I didn't know what was right, wrong, or even real.

Jess and Miss J. each took one of my hands in theirs. Hours went by. Mrs. Anderson set a cup of tea in front of me but it remained untouched on the coffee table.

At some point, Miss J. left and Jess fell asleep by my side. And still I sat there, staring at the television but not seeing it, not hearing it. Eventually dawn filtered in through the large window before my mind could finally absorb everything that had happened.

JESS AWOKE to a string of texts from her father, demanding to know where she was and that she get home. In true Jess fashion, she hadn't bothered to tell her dad where she was. In his true fashion, he hadn't noticed her missing for days.

It was only seven in the morning, but I was in the frigid car taking her home.

"Are you going to school tomorrow?"

She was looking out the passenger-side window, her hand resting on her stomach. "Yeah. I mean, why not?"

"Well, that's the spirit, I guess."

She snorted but kept her focus outside.

"Are you okay?" I asked.

"Yeah. I'm fine. Just thinking of how I'm going to tell Dad."

I nodded even though she didn't see me. I pulled up in front of her apartment building.

"Thanks, Ro." She threw open the door. "Hey. I'm so sorry about everything. Your dad. Mike. Trina." Her shoulders slumped. "Man, life kinda sucks right now, doesn't it?"

I forced a laugh but it was an ugly sound and I swallowed to moisten my throat. "Yup. It does." I thought about my dad and wanted to cry. I thought about Mike and wanted to die. I missed him so bad. But I didn't say anything to Jess. She had enough worries.

"I'll call ya later." Jess got out of the car.

"'Kay." I waved and watched her walk into the apartment building, disappearing through the front doors.

When I got back to the Anderson's, Mike's mom was sitting on the chair in the living room, her eyes planted on my face, unblinking.

"Hi," I said, hesitating at the door. "Is everything okay?" Had Mike gotten into an accident? I froze at the door.

She was sitting with a rigid back and knees pressed firmly together. Her jaw was clenched and her fingers tapped on her knees, the only movement in the entire room.

"We need to talk."

"Okay." My heart beat faster than the drum section at a college football game. I pulled off my boots and coat and forced my feet to walk over to the couch.

"Rowan," she started, "we have provided you with a nice home, haven't we? We have treated you like part of our family, only because you *feel* like part of our family. You are welcome here and always will be."

Her voice started to shake and her fingers were moving almost as fast as my heart. "And you've had quite a life. No one would judge you if you had trouble coping with everything that has happened, especially over the past ten years."

Oh my God. Mike told her about the cutting. She was going to throw me into a psych ward, somewhere I'd enter Rowan Slone and leave a zombie, a medicated, emotionless shell of who I used to be. *God, no.* How could Mike do that?

But I was wrong. It had nothing to do with my cutting. It had everything to do with the drugs she found in my room.

In her hand she held a clear plastic sandwich bag, her bright pink nails almost comical against the white powder lining the bottom. But white powder wasn't the only thing in that bag. There was also a razor blade. I didn't need to lean closer. I didn't need to ask what it was. A razor blade was something I was so familiar with I could almost smell the steel from here.

She didn't need to speak. The question was written all over her face, in the set of her lips, and the purse of her brows. She wouldn't accuse me, though. That much I knew. She would ask and listen.

"That's not mine."

"Do you have any explanation as to how it got into your room?"

"That wasn't in my room. There's no way."

Her eyes were unblinking and her weighted silence made me want to shrink into the floor.

Clearly she'd found that in my room. But how? Mike? Jess? Who else had been in my room?

Trina.

Had Trina left that in my room?

"It has to be my sister's."

"Trina's?" Her voice was matter-of-fact. "When was Trina in your room?"

I shook my head, my mind spinning. "I don't know. I mean. The other day Gran took her upstairs to lie down. The day Dad died. But Trina has been on drugs for a while."

"How do you know? Have you seen her actually doing drugs?"

"No. I mean, yes. We got into a fight in school a week ago. She was high then. And I've seen her smoking a joint."

"You got into a fight at school? Why didn't you tell me?"

My palms started to sweat. "I, um, I don't know. I didn't get into trouble. We were called into the principal's office but that was it. He let me go. He kept Trina. I figured it was because she was high. I don't know." I wrung my shirt in my hands, the razor blade calling to me.

"So, you're telling me that Trina is on drugs and planted this in your room?" She held up the bag and all I could see was the razor. The razor. The razor. The world was spinning around me. I think Mrs. Anderson believed me, but there was enough in her tone to tell me I shouldn't be so sure.

"I would never do drugs. I would never…do that."

She nodded, but it wasn't in the least reassuring. "This is a very big deal, finding drugs in my home. In all my years, none of my children have brought drugs into my home."

"I'm not one of your children," I spat, my control slipping away by the minute.

"No," she breathed. "I guess you are not."

"Those drugs aren't mine. I promise. I would never do drugs, and I would certainly never bring them into your home."

But I would use that razor blade…

"Do you know what kind of drug this is? Is it cocaine?"

I didn't want to step forward, get close to the bag. If I did, I didn't know if I'd have the resolve to not grab that blade and slice a new line in my arm. Trina used it to slice lines of drugs. I used it to carve up my skin. Weren't we a pair worth saving? An ugly burst of laughter, tinged with hysteria, burst from my lips.

"What's so funny?"

I bit the inside of my cheek so hard I tasted blood. "I'm sorry. I mean, I…I'm sorry. I don't know what kind of drug that is. Cocaine or meth. I don't know."

Mrs. Anderson knew my sister. She knew all that Trina was capable of. And I thought she knew me. But there was just enough question lingering behind her bright eyes that made me want to crawl into a corner and hide. Because what I saw there was judgment and a hint of accusation. Like mother like son?

"We'll talk about this later."

I nodded and went upstairs on silent feet. Without changing, I crawled into my bed and pulled the covers over my head.

chapter nineteen

THE NEXT morning when I walked downstairs, I didn't know what was waiting for me. Maybe Mrs. Anderson packed my bags overnight and was ready to throw me out the door. Maybe she had decided I was telling the truth and realized Trina was not someone to be trusted—not now, not ever.

What happened was something in between. She must've heard me coming because she came out of the kitchen just as I stepped into the living room. Her eyes took a minute to study my face. As much as I wanted to look away, I couldn't and found myself studying her in return.

She wiped her hands on a dishtowel and said, "Good morning."

"Hi." I opened the front door and Levi darted out.

"How did you sleep?"

"Good," I lied.

"Rowan..." She laid the towel across the back of the couch. "I just want you to know that I believe you. I was just shocked last night. I have never found drugs before. I wasn't sure what to do."

"It's okay." My shrug belied how much last night had hurt me. "I mean, I'm sure it was a shock."

"Yes." She went to the window and watched Levi roll in the grass. "You are a part of this family, Rowan." She put her hands on my upper arms and tears filled her eyes. "You're like a daughter to me. I don't want this to change anything."

I swallowed against the knot growing in my throat and when she pulled me into her arms, I hugged her back. But just barely, my mind flashing with images of the look in her eyes last night as she held up the bag of drugs.

AFTER LEVI came back in, I made sure his feet were clean and went upstairs to get ready for school. There had been nothing else to say so Mrs. Anderson went back to the kitchen after a quick squeeze of my arm that did little to reassure me.

When I went into my room, my cell phone was ringing.

"Hello?"

"Rowan? It's Mike."

I shut the bedroom door and sat on the bed. "Talked to your mom, I guess?" Was he calling to bawl me out about the drugs?

"No. Why?"

"Nothing." I looked out the window. "What's up?"

"I don't know. I was just thinking. About everything and how it ended."

Ended. Such a permanent word. "Well, it's fine. I mean, everything is fine."

"Is it? I can't get the image of your arm out of my head. It's just, *always there*. I didn't sleep at all last night thinking about it."

I rolled my eyes but kept my voice neutral. His problem with my arm was just that—his problem. "I know, you think I'm *sick*..." I made the word sound like a curse. "But I haven't cut since that day at the hospital."

"But you are sick, Rowan. You need help. What's going to happen the next time something bad happens? Or you get stressed?"

His tone of voice pricked at my nerves like a million needles were sticking me through my clothes.

"Mike, I don't know what your problem is, but it's not my concern. Call me sometime when you feel like talking and not preaching."

"I'm not preaching, but you obviously need someone to step in and take control."

"Stop belittling me, Mike. I'm eighteen. I would be in college like you if I hadn't failed the fifth grade so save the sanctimonious bullshit." I bit my lip. This conversation wasn't going well. I owed so much to Mike; I didn't want us to fight.

"That's all true, but you've gone through a lot."

"I have gone through a lot, but it doesn't mean there is something wrong with me." Somewhere in the middle of this uncomfortable exchange were the two people who had loved each other, loved each other still. I tried to remember that boy who had stolen my heart last year. Right now he was a boy who was about to get a swift kick in the ass if he didn't stop badgering me.

"Rowan." His breath hissed through the line. "I don't want to fight. I still care about you. You should talk to my mom. Maybe start therapy."

If he were standing in front of me, I would've punched him in the face.

"You are such an asshole. Such an ass!" My voice rose. "What is wrong with *you* to sit there and judge *me*?"

"Are you serious? I find out you use your arm as a chopping block, that you've hidden it from me all this time, and you think I shouldn't be upset about it?"

"Yes! That's exactly what I think!" My hands shook and rage tore through me. Or maybe it was despair. He was right. Part of him was right. But I wouldn't admit that he had a right to be upset. Not now. Maybe not ever. I'd done the best I could.

"Are you always going to shut me out?" he demanded.

"Are you always going to treat me as an inconvenience?"

"What?"

I knew I had changed the subject, but I was still upset about how little I'd seen him over the past months. If we were going to fight, we were going to fight over everything that had happened.

"There is no room in your life for me. You went away to college and left me here for your mom to take care of!"

"Rowan, you're acting crazy. I have a scholarship. I can't just run home every weekend!"

"Fine. Then don't bother coming home again." It sounded so foolish. This was his home, not mine. But I couldn't help it. Maybe the last couple of days were getting the best of me.

He was quiet on the other end. Just as panic erupted through me and I was about to plead for him to forget those last words, he said, almost like he was talking to himself, "Maybe we *should*."

"Should what?" I demanded as his words drifted through the air. Then I realized it like a sucker punch to the gut; something I'd known for a while now. "Just say it." I begged him to speak the words and not speak the words, all at the same time.

"Break up."

There. He said it. The silence on the line was so heavy that surely it would send the entire house crumbling to the ground.

"Break up," I repeated.

"Yeah." He sighed heavily. "Maybe for a little while."

I looked out the window, focusing on the numbness coursing through my limbs.

"Maybe if you get into the university next year, we can, you know, see where things are."

"Maybe." My voice sounded robotic, forced.

"I'm sure you can stay on there with Mom and Dad. They like having you there. Tabitha will kill me if you left."

An ugly sound burst out of my lips. "Sounds like you've been thinking about this for longer than just today."

The lack of response on the other end told me he had thought about this, and likely even talked to his parents.

AFTER SCHOOL, for the first time since I left, I drove to my old home. It was strange traveling back down this narrow country road even though everything looked the same as it did the last time I was here.

I almost missed the dirt driveway to my left—maybe it was subconscious, maybe it was sheer accident. But I slammed on the brakes and yanked the steering wheel, making the tires skid. Soon I was parked in front of my childhood home.

Gran's touches were everywhere: there were no broken flower pots lying around with dead weeds hanging over the sides; the front porch had been swept; the shutters were freshly painted. The gutter still hung off the right side of the house, but that would probably cost more money to fix than Gran had.

Feeling like a stranger, I knocked on the door. Almost immediately it swung open.

"You don't have to knock, silly. This is still your home." Gran stood before me in a green sweatshirt and a pair of dark blue jeans. Her sneakers were too white and blaring, but I didn't tell her that.

I passed through the front door and stood in the living room, looking around.

"Come. Sit. I'll get you something to eat."

I didn't resist when Gran pulled my coat off. "Is Trina here?"

"No. She's with her friend, Jennifer. I don't like that girl." Gran hung up my coat. "But it seems like she's Trina's only friend. Of course, boys are calling here all the time. There is no shortage of them."

She veered me toward the chair, the same chair that my dad always sat in. I slipped from her touch and went to the couch.

"Tea? Water? Soda?"

"Nothing. I'm fine."

She narrowed her eyes. "You've lost weight again."

I was suddenly very interested in the worn armrest.

"I'll make you something to eat then."

"No." I looked up. "I don't want anything to eat. Did you say that you had something for me from Dad? I can't stay long. I have to work."

"Oh." Gran's face fell. "Okay. I'll be right back." She shuffled down the hall and into my parents' old room, the room she had taken over after my dad left and my mom went to jail.

She came back moments later carrying a wooden box.

"You won't believe this." She sat beside me, making the couch dip under her weight. I scooted away to put a few inches between us. "But this box," she ran a hand over the closed lid, "your dad made when he was in shop class in high school. He was pretty talented, wasn't he?"

The top of the box had an American flag and an eagle carved into its surface. I ran my finger over the dipped surface.

"He was a really good artist. After he enlisted in the military, though, I don't think he ever did another thing about it. He was good at drawing, painting, woodwork. He had a lot of potential. I think that's why it was so hard when your mom got pregnant."

She opened the box. Inside was a stack of thick papers, folded so they fit. She pulled them out and I could see that they were paintings and drawings.

Gran handed them to me. "These are your dad's things from when he was in high school. His junior year, he won an award for best painting. It was even hung up in the local museum for a year or so." She pulled out a certificate. "Here. This is what it was."

I read the certificate in confusion. I'd never known this about my dad. Were we talking about the same person?

"But here, this is what you need to see." She set the stack of papers aside and laid a single folded sheet in my lap.

When I opened it, I saw a pencil sketch of a baby. It looked like it was at least two months old with a hairless head, chubby arms, and round charcoal eyes. Its lips were opened wide like it was laughing at something that I couldn't see.

Emotion erupted through my body. It was my sweet, little brother right before he died. I started to gasp for breath. Why would Gran show me this? To remind me that the only thing Dad loved, truly loved in the world was Aidan?

There was a blanket drawn around the baby's torso. Did he draw this after Aidan's death? What did this mean? Gran was rubbing my back, right between my shoulder blades, and it was the only thing that kept me conscious. Otherwise, I surely would've gotten lost in the grief.

"Here," Gran said, her voice low. She pointed with a wrinkled finger, her nail long enough to show me exactly where to look.

And I saw it; not the word *Aidan*, but the words *My beautiful Rowan* written in tiny black letters along the hem of the blanket.

"See? He loved you, honey. Always."

I collapsed into my Gran's arms. At some point she eased the paper out of my hand so my tears wouldn't smear the drawing.

What did this mean? My dad had loved me? He'd been happy enough to have a baby daughter that he drew a picture of me? And was it him I was smiling at in the picture?

This changed everything. Everything.

I TOOK the long way to the shelter, even though I was already late. The picture was lying in the passenger seat, my own baby face watching me as I drove. It was strange, unsettling, and freeing all at the same time.

It did cross my mind that Gran had forged those words to make me feel better. I had held the paper close to my face and studied it the entire time she was on the phone with my mom's caseworker. It looked like his handwriting. It seemed to merge with the other lines that made up the drawing. There was no reason to think that it wasn't written by my dad.

Aidan looked a lot like Trina when she was a baby and nothing like me. The more I glanced at the picture beside me, the more I saw my own face as it was in the baby pictures that used to hang on the living room wall. This wasn't Aidan. It was me. *Me.*

Did my mom know about this picture? Surely she did if Gran knew. Mom must have seen a side to Dad that he never showed his daughters. Back when they were in high school and their lives were full of the future and possibility and optimism, did Mom see his talent?

Did he ever draw a picture of her?

It was as if a curtain was being lifted from my eyes. There was more to my dad than I could've imagined. Did the same hold true for my mom? Was my mom more than what she seemed?

My childhood memories overflowed with images of my mom sleeping all day, of my mom shoving candy and pastries into her already fat face, of my mom cowering behind her curtain of dark hair anytime something was expected of her. Was there a different person who used to dwell beneath that unpleasant exterior? Someone who had loved me and who I actually loved too?

Suddenly an idea popped into my head like a little sprout from a long-dormant seedling. Forging a relationship with my mother was not an option right now. Was there another choice, though? Another way to find peace with her?

I pulled the car over to the side of the road, and stared out the window for a long time.

I WAS an hour late when I got to the shelter. Never would I have been late before, but I knew in my heart Janie would understand. She told me after the funeral to take as much time as I needed.

When I walked in, she was with a customer. After a quick glance, she gave me a sympathetic smile and turned back to the older woman standing before her.

I walked down the short hallway toward the dog room. The animals were quiet as I greeted them. "Hi, everyone."

Large eyes looked up at me from the different cages. A few stood and came to the edge, pushing noses as far into the wire as possible. I gave each dog an individual greeting as I made my way back to Charley-bear. He was still shy, unsocialized, scared, and timid, but there was a tenderness to him. I could *sense* it, and that tugged at my heart.

I sat by his crate. "Hi, sweet boy." I put my finger through the opening and rubbed his back. He looked at me with eyes that made my breath catch. It was like he had a human face with human emotions and what these emotions were telling me was that he was sad.

And I hated to see animals sad.

"It's okay. I promise. I am really good at finding homes for our animals. I'll find you a good one."

As quietly as possible so I didn't upset the other dogs, I opened the crate. Charley-bear didn't pull away when I slid my hand in. He jumped slightly when I started to rub his ear the way Levi liked. Within a couple of minutes, he rose to his feet and slowly crossed the small distance toward me.

"It's okay," I whispered. "It's okay."

He came out, putting tentative paws on the cool tile. I kept rubbing his ear because he seemed to like that. Soon he was standing in front of me, his head leaning over my lap. I started on the other ear, too. His head dipped, almost like it was putting him in a trance.

"Good boy," I said.

The other dogs didn't whimper, or bark, or show signs of jealousy. When I looked over at them they were just watching us. I smiled at them all. "Thank you," I choked, so grateful for their understanding in that moment that I would've adopted them all if I could.

When I turned back to Charley-bear, he was sitting. I leaned my face down, something I knew I shouldn't do, but I couldn't help it. I rested my forehead on his as I rubbed.

His breathing was loud, mine was soft. I started to run my hands over his head, down his shoulders, over his back. He tensed a little but after several long caresses, he seemed to relax again.

When I heard Janie's heavy footsteps coming down the hallway, I started to whisper to him. "Janie's coming." My voice was just loud enough to hear, my caresses slow and gentle. "Everything's okay. I promise."

"Rowan?" Janie came into the dog room. She stopped by the door when she saw me. At first her expression flashed with alarm, concern, irritation. Then her shoulders fell and she smiled. "How did you coax our little friend out of there?" She lowered her voice, too.

My hands were steady and consistent, traveling a path from his ears, over his head, and down his back. He was watching Janie, but still seemed relaxed under my touch.

"It was just time, I think." I smiled back at her.

"Well, it is good timing. The lady out front is interested in seeing him. She is a widower who never had children, so there are no young ones to worry about. She is interested in adopting him. I don't think he's violent. Do you?"

I gazed down into his dark eyes, searching, trying to read into his little heart, his tender, damaged soul.

"I don't think he would hurt her." I cleared my throat to try and rid myself of the lump that had formed there. "She wants to see him now?"

"She just left. She wanted to see him now but then received a phone call she had to take. She has to go out of town on business and will be here next week."

That gave me enough time to find out if my idea would work and if it did, we'd have to find this nice widower a different dog.

chapter twenty

"I JUST can't let this lie." Mrs. Anderson stood in the living room, Gran beside her, and Trina slumped on the couch. Mr. Anderson had left that morning for a dental conference otherwise, I'm sure he would've been there, too.

I dropped my bag on the floor. There was no need to ask what she was talking about.

"If they were, in fact, Trina's drugs, your grandmother needed to know."

"They aren't my drugs," she spat from the couch.

"Hush," Gran demanded. "Rowan, come in and sit down so we can get to the bottom of this."

With lead feet, I walked over to the fireplace, my head spinning from déjà vu. It was only months ago that I had been called into the living room of my old home to witness Trina's lie that she'd been raped by Mike. The statement had been untrue then and her statement was untrue now. Would I never be rid of my lying sister?

"Rowan, do you know anything about these drugs?" asked Gran.

"No."

"Neither do I," Trina whined, crossing her arms over her chest.

"Girls, someone brought drugs into this house. I have a mind to go to the police, but I want answers before I decide what to do. Rowan says they aren't hers and I'm inclined to believe her."

Inclined to believe me? I thought that was a done deal.

Trina's blue eyes looked from Mrs. Anderson to Gran and back. She didn't once look at me. Suddenly, she melted into tears.

"I'm so sorry! They're mine. I'm so sorry. It's just been…been so hard!" She hiccupped and covered her face with her hands. "I miss my sister. It's so hard not having Rowan home. She doesn't talk to me. She doesn't act like a sister. I miss her," she wailed. "I miss my sister." Her shoulders shook with the weight of her tears.

I rolled my eyes. Mrs. Anderson looked stunned. Gran watched her with a tilted head as if trying to figure out truth from deception. There was no trying to figure out for me. This was the same old song and dance.

It took approximately thirty seconds before Mrs. Anderson sprang across the room and knelt in front of Trina. A second later, Trina was in her arms, Mrs. Anderson cooing to her in a soft voice. Gran didn't move to comfort Trina. Instead, she came to my side and put a hand on my shoulder.

Her eyes were on my face. After trying not to return her gaze, I finally gave up and looked into her familiar eyes. There was so much there, so much unsaid that didn't need to be said. She believed me. I could tell she did.

But I could only stay there for so long. Eventually, I just walked away. I grabbed Levi's leash and left the house. No one tried to stop me. Mrs. Anderson probably didn't even notice. She and Trina were sitting on the couch with their heads bent together, Mrs. Anderson holding my sister's hand in her own.

Something needed to change. I couldn't stay here any longer. Not after everything that had happened. But where could I go? Where did I belong?

As I walked along the smooth sidewalk, Levi trotting along beside me, I wracked my brain for options. Nothing came to mind as I headed into the dog park. I pulled off Levi's leash and slid his ball out of my pocket. I threw it far across the lawn and he darted after it.

Going back to my home was not an option. Trina was still there. Someday my mom would return.

The Anderson's home was not a good fit anymore. Things had changed. Mike and I had broken up. His mother seemed to be Trina's crusader. I wasn't their child. I wasn't part of their family.

Levi and I stayed at the dog park for an hour and it took that long for another jarring idea to materialize in my head. My mind flipped between this new thought and the one I had had earlier about my mom. If they both worked…if I could make these changes happen, my life was about to take a drastic turn, hopefully for the better.

ON MONDAY, I arrived at school early to see Miss J. The heat in the building didn't seem to be working, and I slid my cold hands into my coat pockets. The door to her office was open and Miss J. was reading the newspaper, wrapped up like she was going for a hike in the snow.

"Hey."

"Hi, Rowan. How are you? I'm glad to see you here. I didn't know if you would come in today or not." She put a hand on her red nose, cupping it around her skin.

"I'm okay." I fell into the chair.

"What's up? You're here early."

"I was just thinking…"

"Yes?"

I paused a minute, gathering my thoughts. The tip of my nose was also cold, and I pushed the back of my hand against it for warmth. "It's freezing in here."

Miss J. had on her winter coat, a thick brown scarf, and gloves. She laughed. "I know. Tomorrow I'm bringing in a space heater. They say we're not allowed to have them, but this is ridiculous." Her eyes widened. "Don't tell anyone I said that. Your guidance counselor doesn't break the rules."

I laughed too even though smiling made my icy cheeks hurt. "I won't tell, I promise."

"So, again I ask, what's up?"

"I don't know." My nerves suddenly exploded. I jumped up and walked to the window, bouncing on my feet for warmth. "Well, maybe I do know."

Outside the window, crossing the parking lot was a girl whose walk and posture reminded me of Jess if it weren't for the pixie-cut blonde hair. But when she drew closer, I realized it *was* Jess. She'd cut her hair, sheering away every trace of the oily black.

Oh my God.

"Rowan?" said Miss J.

She stopped at a picnic table yards from the window where I stood. She didn't sit down, but stretched her arms out wide and yawned.

She wore the tightest shirt I'd seen her wear, showing off the slight bulge to her midsection. Over her sweater, she had on an old black leather jacket that she'd found at Goodwill two years ago.

Ever in true Jess fashion, she still wore her black boots. She would go into labor with those things on. She wore a little black skirt that barely covered her butt, but her thick black tights made it look like she was more covered than she was.

If it weren't for the rounding belly and the newly blonde, short hair, she was the same old Jess. But then she wasn't. And she would never be that girl again. In five months she'd be a mother.

I turned to face Miss J.

"I want to go to Berkeley."

Her brows pursed. "Okay. But I thought you were waiting to see what they'll offer you."

I TURNED back to the window and watched Jess sit down and put earbuds in her ears. "There is an apartment open above you, right? Didn't I see a sign saying it's for rent?"

"Yes... Why? Rowan, you're talking all over the place."

"Jess and I are going to rent that apartment. We'll move in as soon as possible."

"As soon as possible?"

"Yeah. I'll drive over there after school."

Outside the window, Jess closed her eyes and put her hand on her belly.

"Can you afford a place of your own?"

A dingy yellow bus pulled up and a group of students piled out.

"Janie gave me a raise recently. She promoted me to assistant manager. I won't have a lot extra, but with Jess working at the bookstore, we should be okay."

Miss J. was quiet, reading something on her computer screen.

"What are you doing?" I asked.

"I'm double-checking that you can move out and live on your own while in high school."

"Why not?" I demanded. "I'm eighteen. I'm an adult. Right? And Jess will be eighteen tomorrow."

"Technically. But you're still in school, so I need to double-check. I'm sure it'll be fine."

I clenched my teeth as I waited, listening to the sound of her fingers flying across the keyboard. "There."

"What?" I sat back down in the seat and shoved my hands in my pockets.

"I sent an email to the principal to see what he has to say."

I nodded.

"But you know what?"

"What?" I braced myself for the lecture.

"I think that is the best idea you've had all year."

I smiled and even though my cheeks were frozen, my heart felt light and warm.

I DIDN'T say anything to Jess about the apartment.

"I love the hair, Jess. It looks amazing." And it really did. Jess had pretty, soft features when they weren't masked under the makeup and dyed hair.

"Thanks. Well, I thought it was time to, you know, make a change."

"Well, it looks great." I grabbed my textbook and slammed the locker. "Your makeup looks great, too."

For the first time ever, I actually saw Jess blush. Normally she wore so much makeup her emotions were well hidden.

She smiled. "I'm trying something."

"Yeah? What's that?"

"I'm, well, obviously pregnant, and I decided to try to be as healthy as I can be. You know, for this little guy."

"Little guy?"

She bit her lip. "It's a boy."

"What? When did you find out?"

Her smile faded a little. "Last night. My stomach started hurting really bad and I took the bus to the ER."

"Why didn't you call me?"

"Ro, you have enough going on. They did an ultrasound, or whatever it's called."

"And everything is okay?"

"Yep. She said I'm eating too much. Indigestion. And she also said it's a boy."

"A boy! Wow. That's cool."

"I know. I'm actually starting to warm up to this whole idea. You know, being a mom and all." She ran a hand over her belly. "I can't wait to meet him."

"Are you going to tell Paul?"

She shook her head, and I acted like I didn't see the sadness wash over her face. "No. I don't even know where he is. The last time I tried to call his cell, it said it was no longer in service. He's good and gone."

I wove my arm through hers as we walked down the hall. "Well, good riddance to him. We'll be all right—all three of us." She squeezed my arm and we went to class.

AFTER SCHOOL, I had two stops to make before I went to the shelter. Stop one had me driving down the interstate heading toward Berkeley Mountain College. I needed to see if the same feelings I had on my first visit were still there. The same parking space I'd used last time was open so I pulled into it, taking it as a sign.

I stepped out of my car and stood on the curb, watching the bustle of a busy college campus whirl around me. Miss J. didn't think I'd have any trouble being accepted to this school. The only issue would be scholarship money. I always thought that whichever school offered me the most money was the one I'd have to attend. But now with this raise…Well, there might be other options.

Plus, this school was known for giving generous aid to its students. I was local, which was a bonus—many locals didn't come to this school. They often went to the state university where Mike was or to another state school two hours away. This little college mostly pulled international students and ones from other states with wealthy families that could afford to pay the tuition. I hoped, as I stood on that sidewalk, it meant that there would be more funds left over for students like me.

"Hey! I know you."

To my right Shane was walking toward me, his guitar slung over his back. His hair was disheveled and his flannel shirt hung half in and half out of his pants.

"Hi." I took this as another sign, though seeing him wasn't the reason I'd driven over here.

He smiled as he stopped in front of me.

"Rowan," I reminded him.

"Yeah. I remember. Hey, did you decide to come to school here?"

It really was a beautiful campus with the buildings planted atop a soaring mountainside with surrounding peaks that were snow-capped and surreal. It almost looked like a picture from a photography book. The air seemed cleaner, fresher as I pulled it into my lungs. There was a feeling that I had being here the last time. It was this feeling I wanted to see if I had again. And I did. There weren't many ways to describe it other than it *felt right*.

"Maybe. I'm not sure yet."

I stole glances at Shane, trying not to look like I was staring, but I couldn't help it. When he smiled, his deep dimples showed. His teeth were slightly crooked but in a good way.

"You want to grab a cup of coffee? I can show you the student union."

I glanced at the looming clock that sat atop a long black pole. "Sure. I have about twenty minutes. Is that enough?"

"Yeah, sure. I have class soon anyway."

He flicked his head to the side, and I stepped in stride beside him. He was taller than Mike and the top of my head didn't even make it to his shoulder. But he was thinner than Mike. Then, when I realized what I was doing, I bit the inside of my lip. I did not want to start comparing every guy I met to Mike.

I clenched my fists and forced my attention on Shane. "So, have you been playing much?"

"Oh yeah. Every day. I got a gig this coming weekend in a little bookstore near here."

"Where? My best friend works at a bookstore."

He laughed, an easy, effortless sound. "I don't remember the name. It's written down somewhere. What's the name of the place your friend works?"

"Appalachian Books and More. It's in Oak Town."

"That sounds familiar. It might be the same place. Do you know if they're having a music night?"

"I don't know. She hasn't said. If her boss mentioned it, there's a good chance she didn't even hear him. She's not exactly a marvel of concentration."

He laughed again. "In here." He held open a glass door and within a step, I was inside the student union, just like I belonged there. A blast of heat hit me and made my frozen fingers tingle.

Before me sprawled a huge room, long and wide with blaring lights. Along the left side was a small, separate sitting area where a handful of students hunched over books or laptops. A little farther over started a string of little shops—a place to get coffee and four different fast food restaurants. The rest of the room was covered with tables that were half-full with students.

"Coffee is over here. I have to admit, I come in here at least three times a day." He leaned into my ear and dropped his voice low. "I have an addiction." He chuckled and his breath stirred my hair.

"To coffee?" I leaned back toward him as if sharing a secret.

"Yep. To coffee. I'm such a bad boy."

The smile on my face seemed to seep into my bloodstream. "Well, I won't tell anyone."

We poured our coffees—his in the largest cup they had and mine in the smallest. When we went to the counter to pay, he said, "It's on me."

"Oh, thanks, but that's okay. I'll get mine."

He pulled out his worn wallet. "I insist. Consider me the local school representative. If they get tuition out of you because I bought you a coffee, maybe I'll get a better grade in linguistics."

I couldn't help but laugh. He was an easy person to be around. "Well, thank you very much. And if I end up going here, I'll look you up and return the favor."

"That's a plan." With a light tap, he hit his cup against mine. "Cheers."

"Cheers."

"So find out if it's your friend's bookstore and see if you guys can come. I always like seeing a friendly face when I play. Some of my other friends will be there. You met them the other day. The more the merrier. I tend to get a little nervous." His relaxed expression told me otherwise. He didn't seem like someone who let too much stress him out. If I played guitar like him, nothing would stress me out either.

"I will. That sounds like fun. But I have to get going."

"Okay. Well, hey, it was great to see you again. I'm going to forego my gentlemanly duties and stay here to get some work done instead of walking you to your car, if that's okay. It's a pretty safe campus."

"Oh no. You don't need to walk me anywhere. I'm good. Thanks again."

"See you around, Rowan."

"Bye, Shane."

As I walked toward the door of the student union, I looked around. Students seemed so normal here: studying, talking, listening to music, playing cards. It was crowded in this building, and outside on the lawns, but nothing like the university where Mike was.

I couldn't say exactly what made me think that there was something different about this school, but it had a relaxed feel to it that I liked. Hopefully, there was some wiggle room on the scholarship front.

chapter twenty-one

MY NEXT stop had me heading back toward town in the direction of the small county prison where my mom was held. The only time I had been here was during Mom's trial. As one of the main witnesses, I was forced to sit on that wooden chair, raise my right hand, and state that I would tell the truth, the whole truth, and nothing but the truth. I had never been so ready to speak, to free myself from the burden of my past.

But it hadn't left me with any peace. I'd barely been able to choke out my version of the day Aidan died. The judge had to ask me several times to speak up, even though there was a small microphone pointed at my face.

I only looked at Mom once during my testimony. She was crying, her shoulders shaking like she was in a washing machine. Her face was blotchy and red, eyes swollen and glassy. She looked like she had lost some weight, but it was hard to tell.

She watched me as I spoke—I could feel her eyes on me. I put up a barrier to my feelings and told my version of the story in an *as a matter-of-fact tone* as I could muster. Then I left. And I hadn't returned to this square, brick building.

Here I was now, though I wasn't going to visit my mom. There was no part of me that wanted to do that. But I needed to talk to someone at the jail, someone that could help me. There was peace to be brought into this situation if I could just get the right answer. And I'd have to get it. I didn't see another option.

"Can I help you?" A tall, thick woman looked up from behind a desk. She had closely cropped gray hair and wore no makeup or jewelry. The only verification that she was a woman was that her name tag read *Valerie Snow*.

The room had the faint smell of cigarettes and strong coffee. I don't know where the cigarette smell came from, but there were about five cups of coffee sitting around her desk in various levels of fullness.

"Hi." I cleared my throat. "Can I speak to someone about the Prisoners and Pets Program? I work at the animal shelter and we have a pet that we would like to pair with someone who is here. In the jail." My palms started to sweat. Was this the right thing to do? Mom should burn in Hell so why did I want to send her a dog to love and care for?

But it felt right. That was all there was to it.

"That would be me. I'm in charge of that program, though it's been stagnate lately." She leaned back in her chair and fixed her eyes on my face. "Talk to me." She twisted a plain gold wedding band around and around her finger.

"I um..." I started to cough. "Excuse me."

"Would you like a mint?" She picked up a hard candy.

"Um, no thank you. We, well, we have a dog that has been neglected. He's been in the shelter and he doesn't seem to be violent but needs love and attention."

"Okay. That sounds good. We have several prisoners here now, though not a full house. I think we have a couple of good options that come to mind."

"Well, I think there is someone...I mean, there is someone in particular that I think would be a good fit for this dog."

Her thin brows rose. "Who?"

"Amy Slone."

Her eyes narrowed. "What's your name?"

"Rowan," I whispered. "Rowan Slone."

"Ah-ha. I thought I recognized you."

I didn't recognize her, but that didn't matter. Mom's trial had been a whirlwind, most of which I didn't remember and didn't ever want to remember again.

My hands grew restless under her gaze and I fidgeted with the zipper of my coat.

"Okay. I think that's a great idea. Your mother is doing very well—"

But before she could continue, I shook my head so hard it nearly gave me whiplash. "I don't…"

"Oh. I understand. Okay. Let me take down your information." She gave me a sympathetic smile that almost made her angular, masculine face beautiful. "I know Janie. We go way back." She slid a piece of paper to me over the desk. With shaky hands, I wrote down my name and the shelter's number.

"Thank you." I slid the paper back toward her.

"You're welcome. Thanks for coming in. I believe in this program and the good it can do."

I nodded and walked out. My knees barely carried me to my car and shook the whole way to the shelter.

"Hi, Janie."

"Hey, Rowan. How was your day?"

"It was good actually. No complaints." I set my backpack behind the counter.

Janie fiddled with a strap on her blue overalls and then pulled her long hair up into a ponytail. "If you want to go home and take a little more time off, that's fine. I'm okay here."

"I appreciate that but this is one of the few places I love to be."

"Oh, I understand that. I love these animals. We got a new dog in today. An old one."

"Why did they bring him in?"

"The owner is going overseas for work. He said there was no one to take him. The dog is really sweet and seems gentle. Such a shame."

"How old is he?"

"Ten."

I shook my head, my heart hurting for the dog. Someone wouldn't give up their child if they had to move, and I knew Janie agreed from the look on her face.

"He seems fine, though, and will make a good dog for someone else. We'll go through the usual procedures before we put him up for adoption but I don't foresee a problem."

"I'm glad to hear that." And I was. Maybe there was an even better home for the dog out there. Maybe an elderly couple who were home most of the time and would want the companionship. Maybe the lady who'd come in the other day interested in Charley-bear.

Janie started toward the back rooms, but I stopped her. "Janie, can I ask you something?"

"Sure. Anything." She walked back to the counter and leaned on one end. I leaned on the other. We looked like two misfits at the saloon waiting on our foaming beers.

"Um, well, I had an idea. And I think it's a really good one. But I need your guidance and, of course, your permission."

"Okay."

I didn't know why I was suddenly so nervous. Janie was about the easiest person in the world to talk to. She'd never said a negative or judgmental thing that I'd ever heard. Everything I knew about her told me she would like this idea. Then why was I anxious?

Because I needed this to work. There was no room for a relationship with my mom. Not now. Maybe not ever. But after Dad dying, I needed to do *something*.

So I pulled in a deep breath and said, on the exhale, "You know that dog, Charley-bear? The timid one who is just starting to come around?"

"Yes."

"And, um, do you know about that program Prisoners and Pets?"

"Yes. I'm familiar with it. The prison used to contact us for dogs but hasn't in a couple of years or so. Why? Do you think Charley-bear would be a good pet to consider?"

I nodded and picked at the edge of the counter. "I do. And…" I swiped my hand across the clean surface.

"Rowan? Spit it out. There is no idea that is a bad one."

Another inhale. "I would like to try to, I mean, I think Charley-bear would be a good fit for my mom."

"Your mom?" She sounded shocked.

"Well, my mom is in jail there."

She nodded. "I had heard something like that, but I didn't know if it was true or not."

"It's true." I cleared my throat. "She might get some benefit and Charley-bear might, too."

Janie bobbed her head up and down while she gazed out the window. Even though it was a cold evening, soon the temperature would warm and little eager buds would sprout into beautiful dogwood flowers on the tree right outside the door.

"Let me think about this," she said. "Although I think it sounds like a great idea, I need to know a little more about your mom to make sure that Charley-bear will be safe. And then we need to do a little more socialization with Charley-bear to make sure he's safe. But this may very well be a good fit and a new way to energize this program."

She looked back at me. "I knew I promoted you for a reason, Rowan. Excellent idea." She started toward the back. "Excellent idea," she said again as she passed out of view.

IT WAS late when I left the shelter. Janie and I didn't talk about my idea anymore, but I did hear her on the phone at one point and it sounded like she was talking to someone at the prison. Despite my curiosity, I didn't want to eavesdrop so I had forced my feet to carry me back down the hall.

This had to work. It was the only way. Nothing else would matter if this didn't work. If it did, it may very well be the thing that sent me catapulting forward, unlocking my future.

I had a hard time concentrating as I drove to the Anderson's. There were several balls in the air, popping like kernels in my head. Charley-bear. Mike. Living with the Andersons. Leaving the Andersons. Jess. So many pieces to the puzzle that I couldn't keep it all straight.

As I stood at the front door of the Anderson's, a shiver washed over me. Something was wrong. Off. The hair on the back of my neck stood. I opened the door and knew immediately what it was.

Trina and Mrs. Anderson were sitting on the sofa, mugs in hand. If I didn't know better, I'd think they were mother and daughter sharing a heartfelt chat over the trials and tribulations of life's many paths. It was one of the most horrifying sights I had ever seen, and I gasped. Had the drug incident led to this? To the two of them spending quality time together? To Mrs. Anderson swooping in to save my sister like she had saved me?

Mrs. Anderson's head whipped around. "Rowan! I'm so glad you're home." She set the cup on the table and hurried to me, her eyes overly bright. "Your sister is here."

Trina plastered a wide smile on her face.

"I see that." Levi sat a few feet away from Trina, staring at her with a less than welcoming expression.

"After the other day, I told her she should come over so we could talk more about what happened."

My lips were firmly pressed together as my stomach knotted in cramps. This was not a scene I wanted to see.

Mrs. Anderson put her arm around my shoulders. For the first time ever, I tensed when she touched me. She dropped her arm. Silence plummeted into the room.

Several moments passed before Mrs. Anderson spoke. "We were just talking. Won't you join us?" She waved toward the couch with one hand while the other hovered at my back but not touching me.

"No, thank you." I struggled to keep my tone respectful. "I'm tired."

"Won't you stay a minute, Sis? I've missed you."

Trina would say anything to lure out Mrs. Anderson's sympathy. Couldn't Mike's mom see this? See what a fraud she was?

"You know that youth group I told you Trina's been going to?" Mrs. Anderson rubbed her hands together. "We wanted to see if you'd be interested in going with her this week. There are a lot of kids from the high school and the college who come to it. There are dances, movie nights, discussions—anything you can think of. This week it's bowling." Mrs. Anderson looked between Trina and me. "I think it would be a good start for the two of you. To start healing…" Her voice dropped off to a whisper. "Spend some time together." She cleared her throat. "I've talked to Trina about her drug use. It seems she uses to make herself feel better."

Trina stood. Levi growled so low Mrs. Anderson didn't seem to notice, but I heard it. And Trina must've heard it too because she glanced at my dog and took a step away from him.

"Ro, would you want to go with me? To the next meeting on Wednesday?" She moved to Mrs. Anderson's side. "It would be good for us." Mrs. Anderson put her arms out, this time touching me with one hand on my shoulder and one hand on Trina's, like she was the bridge of peace and forgiveness.

I slid out of her grasp and went to Levi's side. "I'm pretty busy with work and school. I don't think I have enough time."

Mrs. Anderson watched me for several seconds then nodded. She led Trina toward the door. "I agree with you that it's time to move on, to forgive."

"Thank you so much, Mrs. Anderson. I really appreciate you being so helpful. It is so nice to have someone who cares." Trina shot me a glare that lasted a split second and then disappeared. "Can I come back again?"

"Sure, sweetheart. You have my number. Give me a call if you need anything." She touched Trina's arm. "We can get through this."

Trina hugged Mrs. Anderson and left without even a glance in my direction but satisfaction was written all over her face. Mrs. Anderson locked the front door.

"Honey, she really seems to want to move on; she's sorry for what she did last year. She seems to want to move away from drugs and such. And I really do think she misses you."

I wanted to scream. How could Mrs. Anderson forget that Trina had accused her son of rape? Of getting her pregnant? Had brought drugs into her home? Was she *that* devout of a Christian?

"I'm sorry, Mrs. A., but I have a headache. I'm going to go to bed if that's okay."

Mrs. Anderson sighed and her shoulders stooped. She didn't say anything else, but I could feel her eyes on me as Levi followed me up the stairs. I had never been rude to Mrs. Anderson except I couldn't stomach what I'd just seen. Couldn't stomach it at all.

I locked the door behind me and fell on the bed. Exhaustion weighed me down like I was a stone incapable of moving. I couldn't even get back up to brush my teeth or get ready for bed. With Levi and Scout by my side, I tumbled into a heavy, deep sleep, clutching a piece of paper with a phone number on it.

chapter twenty-two

SIXTEEN HOURS later I woke up to light streaming in through the window, my head groggy from sleep. I went to the bathroom, brushed my teeth, and splashed cold water on my face.

When I got back into the room, I pulled out my cell phone. There was a missed call notice, no voice mail, but a text from Mike. The text read:

> Can we talk?

There were several calls from Miss J. followed by two of her texts:

> Call me. I have news.

She has news? I bit my lip.

Another text:

> Are you not awake yet? Call me.

Was it good news?

It must be good news.

Please let it be good news.

It took two tries to hit the *call back* button.

"Rowan, it's about time!" She sounded like she'd had too much coffee.

"Sorry. Yesterday was a long day." I didn't come right out and ask why she'd wanted me to call. If I was wrong and it wasn't the news I wanted, I could wait to know that.

"Something came in the mail."

"Did you open it?"

"No. Do you want to meet so I can give it to you?"

"No. Open it. Which school is it from?"

"Berkeley."

My breath caught.

"And Rowan, it's a thick envelope. I have a good feeling about this." Her voice rose and dipped like she was singing.

"Open it!" Her excitement was contagious. I closed my eyes and dropped to my knees beside the bed. It seemed like hours passed as I heard the envelope rip and papers rustle.

Oh no. I didn't get in. She's taking too long to tell me. Or I got in but they didn't offer me a scholarship. My heart stopped beating.

"You got a full ride."

I fell over onto the carpet.

"Rowan? Are you there? Full ride to Berkeley Mountain College. Did you hear me?"

"I heard you." My voice was a whisper, muffled by the carpet.

"Congratulations! I knew you could do it."

She always did have faith that I could do it. It was me who wasn't sure.

I started to cry.

SOMETIME LATER, I hung up with Miss J. and pulled out the piece of paper that she had given me yesterday. There was a number written on it and I dialed with shaky fingers.

"Hi," I said when the person on the other end picked up. "I'm interested in the two-bedroom apartment for rent. Has anyone taken it?" I already sounded older, more adult-like. I could see the next four years laid out before me with a clear, golden path lighting the way.

I chewed the end of my pen as I listened. When I hung up, I skipped down the stairs. No one was in the kitchen, so I darted in and grabbed a granola bar to eat on the way to school, feeling hunger pains for the first time in months.

I LOOKED for Jess but she hadn't bothered to come to school again. During study hall, I sent her a text.

Are you okay?

She didn't respond. I stepped outside and called her cell. She didn't pick up. Worry scratched at my good mood and hung with me the rest of the day. After two more texts and two more phone calls, I left after school and drove to the bookstore. Even if she hadn't gone to school, there was a good chance she would be at work. She loved being around books as much as I loved being around animals.

As I drove down Main Street, I saw her walking down the sidewalk. Her head was bent down, hands shoved in her pockets, and her blonde hair was covered by a hood.

"Jess!" I called out my window, pulling into a parking space.

She stopped and peered at me from the side of the hood. Her cheeks were streaked with black eyeliner and mascara. Red lipstick was smeared over her skin, making her look like a demented doll. After seeing her with softer makeup the other day, it was a shock to see her back this way.

"What's wrong?" I demanded, panicked.

She wiped her nose with her hand. "I talked to Paul."

"Yeah?"

"He's not coming back."

My eyes narrowed. "But, Jess, didn't we already know that?"

Tears wove clear paths over the black streaks. She clenched her lips and shook her head. I realized she had never lost hope that he would come back. I hadn't held that same feeling, but I should've known that she would.

"He told you he's definitely not coming back?"

She hiccupped. "He said he found a job. And he's started seeing someone else. Someone closer to his age."

My hatred of Paul multiplied ten times over. "Did he say anything about the baby?"

"Prove it."

"He said *prove it*?"

"He told me to prove the baby is his and then he'll talk about child support. And I even told him it was a boy." Her knees buckled, and she curled down over her knees. "Oh my God. What am I going to do?"

I crouched down and put my arms around her. My own tears fell into her hair. "I'm so sorry, Jess."

"I'm going to have to tell Dad. He's going to kill me."

"Jessica? Are you okay?" A male voice boomed over our heads. Mr. Sumners was standing over us, his paunch belly rounder than it was the last time I saw him.

Jess wiped her eyes and stood. Her boss looked from her to me and back again. Jess, her hands shoved back in her pockets, pulled her jacket open, revealing the swell of her belly. "I'm pregnant."

He stared at her a moment. "I see." He looked at me but said nothing. "Does your father know?"

She snorted. "No. Not yet. I'm sure you'll hear him yelling all the way down here when he finds out."

Mr. Sumners put his hands to his mouth and blew warm air into them. "Come inside. I'll make some tea. Decaf."

We followed him through the door of the bookstore, a blast of overly warm air hitting us in the face. There were even more books inside than the last time I was here, lining the walls in thigh-high piles that made the walkway so narrow, I was surprised Mr. Sumners could weave his way through.

He led us to the back where he had a small kitchen, or rather, one small spot cleared just enough for a hot pot. Even this counter was covered with books—old Stephen King novels, the spines cracked and faded, and one stack of steamy romance novels. I smirked at the thought of Mr. Sumners having a cup of tea and reading one of *those* stories.

"Why don't you two go sit in the cozy chairs up front, and I'll bring you something warm to drink."

We wove our way back toward the front where there were two chairs, the upholstery faded and torn at the edges. There was a fireplace whose black pit was full of ancient-looking encyclopedias. I doubted Mr. Sumners planned to burn them, but they did look like a pile of aged wood.

The store seemed empty unless there was some quiet introvert tucked back in one of the dark aisles. In this place, you could never tell. Of course, it was usually Jess who was huddled in a far corner, sneaking a few moments to read.

Today, though, Jess' eyes weren't focused on a book. Rather, they were bright and glassy behind her glasses. Tears filled them and fell over red-rimmed lids, coursing down her thawing cheeks.

"Jess, it'll be okay—"

"But how?" she interrupted. "Paul is gone. I'll never see him again. Dad will kick me out. I can't support myself, much less a baby. How is it going to be okay?" Jess started to sob, her nose running, her lips quivering. Up to this point, the baby had seemed like a dream, something a little unreal. But right now, with my best friend crying beside me, it seemed very real. Very real indeed. "What was I thinking—wanting to keep it? I'm a fool."

I reached over and took her hand. Her nails were still bare, long and a healthy pink.

I pulled in a deep breath. "It will be okay because I know what you're going to do."

"What?" She was heaving and placed a hand on her chest to help calm down.

"I have a birthday present for you."

She snorted. "I'd forgotten all about my birthday."

"You and I are going to get an apartment together."

Her mouth fell open. "What?"

"There is an empty apartment above Miss J's. It has two bedrooms and the rent is cheap enough that we should be able to pay it. I got an email last night from Miss J. She thinks she can get some agency or something to help with the deposit and first month's rent. This place can also help with groceries if we need it, and they also have formula for," I glanced at her stomach, "you know. The baby."

"You're serious?"

"Dead."

Jess was quiet for several minutes. "Oh my God, Ro. You're serious."

I laughed, feeling almost giddy. Something was changing—I could feel it. The air was different, sweeter, cleaner, warmer. My heart was light and full of *something* good.

Maybe it was knowing that I was making the right decision. After so many months of not knowing where I belonged, finally I knew with a certainty that took the ten tons from my shoulders and tossed them over the precipice.

"But, aren't you going to the university? What about school? You *have* to go to school."

Before I could give her my good news, Mr. Sumners walked in carrying two chipped teacups with roses and vines painted all over the ivory surface. They rested upon dainty little matching saucers.

"Thank you." I took the one he handed me.

Jess took the other. "Thanks, Mr. Sumners. I really appreciate it."

He didn't sit down—there was no other chair—but he put his hands on his hips and said, "So, you're pregnant."

Jess let out a little burst of laughter; a foreign sound in the midst of the silence. "Yep. I'm pregnant."

"When is the baby due?"

"May."

"You've been to see a doctor?"

"Yes."

"Okay." Just as his mouth opened to ask another question, the bell rang, signaling a new customer. "Sit tight and enjoy your tea."

We were quiet for a few minutes as we listened to Mr. Sumners talk to the customer about a box of old comic books he'd gotten from a book convention. Not usually his cup of tea, he was saying, but he thought someone might enjoy them. Then we heard two pairs of footsteps take off toward the back of the store.

I leaned over the armrest toward Jess. "I'm going to start at Berkeley Mountain College. They offered me a full ride. I'll worry about veterinary school when the time comes. I have to get through undergrad first."

"Ro! That's amazing!" She set her teacup down and pulled me into a tight hug over the arms of the chairs.

"So it's perfect. I'll go to school nearby, stay on at the shelter, and we can get an apartment together."

"We'll live together? You and me…and *it*?" She inhaled deeply. I could almost see the air filling her lungs, her limbs, her cells. She placed her hands on her stomach. They rounded against the swell of the baby. "You and me and *him*?" She opened her eyes and looked at me.

"You, me, and him," I answered.

chapter twenty-three

JESS AND I signed the rental contract that night. They scrutinized my driver's license as if they didn't believe I was eighteen, going so far as to ask me my birth date even though it was imprinted on the hard plastic. They never said a word to Jess even though today was her actual birthday. I guess thirty years from now I'd be happy to look younger than I was. Finally, after the guy helping us called in his manager to double-check my license, we left, a new rental contract in hand.

After I dropped Jess off at her apartment, I drove around. I wanted to gather my thoughts before I went back to the Anderson's. Halfway out of town, my phone rang.

"Hello?"

"Rowan?"

I slammed on the brakes before I hit the truck in front of me. "Mike?"

"How are you?"

"I'm, um…" As the word *good* formed on my lips, I sighed. I was about to share with him my morning and remembered the judgment written all over his face the last time I saw him, the last time we spoke. In the end, I said nothing.

"Rowan, talk to me."

"Why are you calling?"

"To tell you I'm sorry. I have been a complete ass. I shouldn't judge you. You say it's in the past, it's in the past."

"Wow," I managed, my head spinning.

"I don't know what came over me. I mean, I've missed you, I guess. It's not easy being away from you. And this team, well, it's hard. Ya know what I mean?"

I nodded.

"Ro?"

"Yes," I said. "I know what you mean."

"I guess it's all just gotten to me. And..." he paused and I could hear his breath through the phone line—"How did I not know? How did I miss that?"

Something in him sounded different—like he wasn't judging me but was judging himself.

"I wasn't that distracted, was I? That I didn't notice you were struggling?"

"No." I didn't want to talk about this, but I guess I needed to. "I am a master at covering it up."

"Was I ever not there for you when you...when, you know, you needed someone? And did that instead?"

I thought back to the times I had cut, when I was eleven...thirteen...when I was seventeen, all the times in between. The cutting had nothing to do with him. He wouldn't have been able to help me even if I'd reached out to him. Or, maybe he would've. But I hadn't given him a chance and that wasn't his fault.

"No. Mike, it was just something I did. But I don't anymore. I started doing it a long time ago before I ever met you."

He was so quiet I pulled the phone away from my ear to see if we were still connected. I was stuck behind a truck but I didn't pass it. Somehow the slow, crawling pace helped settle my thoughts, and my heart.

"Well, I just wanted to say I'm sorry."

"Wow," I said again. This was the Mike I knew. He was not judgmental. He was caring and tender. "Um, thank you. I really appreciate that."

Silence hung heavy for a few minutes and I put my foot on the brake as the truck in front of me pulled onto the off-ramp. It was quiet on the other end of the phone. There were no other voices, no girls squealing or getting sick from drinking too much; no guys demanding he get off the phone and join the party. Why couldn't he find these quiet rooms during our other conversations?

"Where are you?" I asked.

"In the dorm. My roommate is at the clinic. He picked up some sort of disease from the girl he was dating."

"Ew." I cringed.

He laughed. "Yeah. She was a real skank."

"Skank? Is that proper English?" I laughed, too.

"Yep. It's in the dictionary. I'd show you if I actually owned a dictionary."

"That's okay. I'll take your word for it."

"Rowan? I meant it when I said I miss you, and I just wanted to hear your voice. I just wanted to call and say *hi*. We can still do that, right?"

It took several minutes and punching the gas to make the car go as fast as my heartbeat, but I finally answered, "Right. That would be nice."

"God, Rowan, I don't know. I mean, what happened?"

I swallowed against the burn in my throat.

"You don't have to answer. I mean, I know it was my fault. I really screwed things up." He coughed then said, "But anyway. Tell me what's new."

"Now that's a loaded question." I said a silent *thank you* to him for changing the topic. I wasn't sure how I felt and wasn't ready to find out.

"How so?"

I paused, listening for background noise and when I still didn't hear any, I started talking like I wished I had so many times before when the words just would not come. "A lot has been going on. I'm not sure where to start."

"I have nothing but time. Let's hear it."

It took a minute to sink in that I had his attention—all of his attention—and I *really* loved that feeling. "Well, first of all..." And for the next five minutes, I filled him in on Trina and the drugs. His mom hadn't told him, which surprised me. Then I went on to the next topic without stopping for breath. "I was promoted to assistant manager at the shelter."

"That's amazing! Congratulations!"

"Thanks. I'm so excited. And well, it's perfect, because I just heard back from college."

"University? You got in, right?" His tone rose in excitement.

"Um, no." I frowned—our conversation was going so well. But he needed to know that my decision was made. "I got a full ride to Berkeley Mountain College."

His voice was soft when he asked, "Is that where you're going to go?"

It was my turn to be quiet. Finally I breathed out and said, "Yes. That's where I'm going to go. I'm moving in with Jess. We're going to get an apartment together."

"You're moving out of the house?"

"Yeah. It's time. I mean, I can't stay there forever. You and I both know that."

"Sure you can." His voice was strained.

"You know I can't. You and I are no longer together. I'm eighteen and graduating soon. It's time to move on. And after this stuff with the drugs..." I didn't say that I couldn't imagine staying there any longer. Not now. The time had come to move on.

"When are you moving?"

"In two weeks. The beginning of the month."

Our conversation went on another hour. At some point I pulled off the interstate and started down a winding two-lane road that meandered through the countryside. I filled him in on every detail of the past few months, everything he'd missed because he was away and too busy, everything I hadn't told him because the connection between us had seemed lost.

When we hung up there was no talk of our relationship and it was strange—there didn't need to be. The shadow of our last conversation still hung over me like a black cloud. But somehow, I felt closer to him than I had in months. What that meant for us, I didn't question. I just let the feelings warm my heart as I flipped the phone shut and drove back to the Anderson's.

I sat in the driveway for several minutes. Something was changing—maybe it was me, maybe it was just life. But it was time to help that change along so I got out of the car and fought for the courage to do what I needed to do—talk to Mrs. Anderson.

It was no surprise that she was waiting for me, sitting perched on the edge of the couch, her back straight, her face a mixture of understanding and sadness. There had been enough time while I was driving back for Mike to call her and when I saw the look on her face, there was little doubt that he had.

"Oh, Rowan. Come sit." Her eyes were glassy as she patted the seat beside her. Delilah was in the chair, curled into herself. Levi walked over and lay down at my feet. I leaned over and rubbed his ear. "What's going on?"

"You've talked to Mike?"

"Yes. But I'm still not sure what's going on. Is everything okay? I thought you were happy here."

"I am." I looked around the familiar living room, at the house that had become my home. "Moving in here was the best thing that ever happened to me. But it's time. I'm ready to be on my own."

"Does this have anything to do with Mike?" She put a hand on my knee. "It doesn't matter to me and Mr. Anderson that you're no longer together. You are welcome to stay here as long as you need and Mike agreed."

"I know. I do know that."

"Is it Trina?"

I closed my lids and let words swirl around in my head, trying to pick out the ones that were truthful but not hurtful. In the end, I didn't have to.

"I understand," she said. "It was a difficult position to put you in. I thought I was helping, that I could help mend that relationship." She squeezed my knee. "I think I was wrong."

A forced smile pulled at my lips. I didn't want to talk about Trina. That ship had sailed.

"Where are you going to go?" she asked. Delilah trotted over to me. I wrapped my arms around her solid body and pulled her into my lap. She licked my face with her pink tongue, and I laughed.

"I'm going to get an apartment with Jess. She needs me. She, um, well…"

"What's wrong with Jess?" In true Mrs. Anderson fashion, she was immediately filled with concern.

I rubbed Delilah's chin, and she licked me again. "She's pregnant."

"Pregnant? Jess?"

"Yeah. Her dad doesn't know yet, but she's starting to show. And her, well, the father is gone. He's probably not coming back."

"Oh my." She put her hands to her cheeks.

"So we'll live together. Actually there is an apartment for rent above Miss J.'s place. It'll be fine. It'll be good actually."

"And what about college? Are you going to move out when it's time to go to the university?"

"Well, that's another change. I'm going to go to Berkeley Mountain College."

"Berkeley College? Really? I didn't even know that was a consideration."

"It is…has been."

She stared at me for several minutes, and then looked at the floor. "You'll still be close? I'll like that."

So this was what it was like when a mother was concerned for a child. I wasn't Mrs. Anderson's child, but she had such a kind heart, she treated me as one. As for my own mom, well, I'd never know what it felt like to have a mother's care if it hadn't been for Mrs. Anderson.

"I'll be close. And I'd like to keep in touch if that's okay," I said.

I could tell she wanted to hug me, and finally, she couldn't resist. I was pulled into her arms with such force that I was powerless to resist. But I wouldn't have anyway. I wrapped my arms around her and held on tight. To say I would miss her was an understatement.

"Thank you," I choked, tears swelling in my throat. "For everything."

"Sweet girl, you are so welcome."

"I love you." The words surprised me but the fact that it was true didn't.

"I love you, too," she said into my hair.

SCOUT WATCHED me from the pillow, curled into a ball of fur. Delilah sprawled out at the foot of the bed looking bored and uninterested, though her large eyes were focused on my movements. Levi followed me as I walked around the room, going from the dresser to the closet and back again. Every few minutes he would lick my fingers and I would pet his head.

This room, this house, had become my safe zone; Mike and his family my salvation. Where would I be if they hadn't taken me in? Would I still be in that run-down home where the shadows of my childhood were a permanent fixture on the walls? Would I be in the hospital sharing a room with Trina, both of our wrists cut, bleeding, our souls dying?

Emotions washed over me in a wave—gratitude, love, sadness, pain...gratitude. It came back to gratitude. It wasn't the people who should have helped me through life—not my mom, Dad, sister. But it was someone else. And that was okay. Life didn't have to look like a fairy tale for it to be beautiful.

I ran a hand over the dresser where my things still rested—the ring and earrings Mike had given me, my hairbrush, makeup Mrs. Anderson and Tabitha had taught me how to use. In the mirror that hung just behind it, I studied my reflection.

My face, shoulders, and arms were still too thin. Maybe I always would be just a wisp of a girl. No, a wisp of a woman. But if that was me, wasn't that okay?

I tousled my hair and let it fall around my face and shoulders. The person looking back at me was beautiful. Tears welled in my eyes. Mike and his family had helped me see the beauty inside of me.

And the strength.

I could handle this. I was surrounded by people who supported me—Jess, Miss J., Mrs. Anderson, Gran, Janie, my animals. Life would turn out okay.

Life may even turn out to be pretty darned good. My stomach was knotted with little flutters erupting in spurts when I thought about the changes coming my way.

With a deep breath, I closed my eyes, put my palms together, and did something I rarely did—I prayed. I prayed to God, to spirits, to whoever rested just beyond my sight.

I prayed for guidance and more strength. And then I did the most important thing. I said, *thank you.* My life could've turned out far different. True, it could've turned out better. But it could have also turned out worse.

Thank you for all that I've been given.

Chills ran up and down my arms like a ghost or a spirit had caressed my skin. I opened my eyes and gazed into the gray orbs in front of me. And I smiled. Then with a deep breath, I went into the closet and pulled out my old, worn-out suitcase, its edges frayed; the same one that Mike had packed for me when I moved into his home.

I laid it on the bed and flipped it open. Soon the empty pit was filled with my clothes. That night even though I had two weeks until I could move into the apartment, I packed my things. It was time to move on, to move forward.

epilogue

"YOU DID it!" Miss J. hugged me tight. It was a warm day in May with the sun's rays showering the football stadium in golden light.

For a moment I was speechless. I looked around at my classmates, clad in red robes, red caps, and broader smiles than I'd seen during any day at school. Jess was nearby talking to Janie, Angel, and Mr. Sumners.

Her stomach pushed against the cheap fabric of the robe and she rested one hand on the small of her back, but she was smiling, rubbing her belly with her other hand like she was searching for good luck. The baby was due seven days ago, but nothing had happened. Maybe she would have the baby tonight. The apartment was ready. She seemed ready. Now we just needed *him* to be ready.

I looked at Miss J. "I can't believe it, but you're right—I did it."

She nodded. Even Miss J.'s smile was brighter than it had ever been within the dark halls of the school. "So, now what?"

I knew *now what* but I wasn't ready to tell. I would show her later. She *did* live in the apartment below me, after all.

"This or that." I waved a hand in the air. "I have a few errands to run." A group of kids behind me busted out in a song and dance so awful it was perfect, and I laughed.

She nodded. "Now that you've graduated and you're no longer a student, maybe you and Jess can come down later and have a cup of tea."

My lips spread wide. "Great. We'll be there."

"Perfect."

It might seem weird to start hanging out with my old guidance counselor but during my senior year, and especially after living above her for the past several months, I'd already started to think of her as a friend.

I gave her a quick hug. "I'm going to head out now."

She nodded, and I started to walk away. "Hey, Rowan."

I turned.

"You can call me Tanya now."

"ROWAN?" GRAN touched my shoulder and I turned.

"Hi, Gran."

"Congratulations, honey. I am so proud of you."

I smiled and it wasn't forced at all. "Thanks, Gran."

"I have a little something for you." She handed me a white envelope. "Please open it."

With my thumb, I ripped through the flap and pulled out a check written for more money than I could've ever imagined. I thrust it back at her. "No." I shook my head.

She folded my fingers over the check. "Please." Her voice cracked. "I have led a thrifty life. I don't need this for retirement."

"I appreciate it, but this is too much."

"It's not. There is still plenty left."

I shook my head again, not quite comprehending.

"Rowan, you have overcome so much. I think you are an incredible person and if I can give you just a little bit of help, please let me do that. It doesn't make amends for the past but maybe it can help with your future. And sweetheart," she put a hand on my cheek, tears filling her eyes, "it's going to be such an amazing future."

Speechless, I let her pull me into her arms where she held me for a long, long time.

I SHIFTED on my feet, waiting at the counter of the small shop. The walls were painted red and covered in abstract prints of skulls, crossbones, dragons, and devilish imps. The floor was covered in checkered red-and-black tile. There were four large black leather chairs, two on each side of the room. Along the wall were waist-high cabinets with multiple drawers.

"Can I help you?" A man nearly twice my height and three times my weight walked up to the counter on heavy feet.

I tried not to look afraid, uncertain. This was the answer; the next step. If I was really ready to move on from the past, I had to deal with the scars. They may never heal, emotional or physical, but I could turn them into a powerful reminder of what I had overcome.

"I'm here for a tattoo."

His eyes narrowed. "How old are you?"

I pulled out my ID. "Eighteen. Old enough."

He grunted in reply and slid the ID off the counter into his beefy hand. He pulled it all the way up to his eyes, as if he needed glasses but wouldn't wear them.

"Doesn't look fake but if you're eighteen, then I'm the Prince of Wales."

I hardened my stare. "I'm eighteen. Are you going to help me or not?"

"Do you know what you want?" He tossed the ID onto the counter.

He was a bald man, wearing a white T-shirt that was pulled thin over his belly bulge and a black leather vest with silver studs on the shoulders. Tattered jeans hung low on his hips and a silver chain hung from one pocket.

I watched him as he watched me. Finally, I shook off my hoodie. Wearing short sleeves for the first time in years, I thrust my arm out. "I need to cover these. *All* of these."

He gasped, a strangely feminine sound from his thin lips. "My God, kid. Why'd you do that? Your mom not love you or somethin'?"

I let my arm fall to my side. "No. My mom did not love me. Not in the way I needed. Nor did my dad either for most my life. And I have a sister who is psycho and a drug addict. Do you want to hear my life story or should we get on with it?"

"We'll get on with it. Come on." He walked toward a black chair. "Let's figure out what we can do to cover up those ugly scars."

I followed him and plopped down on the chair, scooting my butt back. The chair nearly swallowed me and my feet dangled off the end. He pulled out three white binders. He sat two on the small cabinet, pulled up a backless stool, and brought one binder to me. He opened it up and said, "Let's see what our options are."

"I know what I want, and we won't find it in those binders."

WHEN I left the shop, the sun was still shining bright overhead. My arm throbbed like I'd been stung by a hundred tiny bees but compared to the pain I'd put myself through those years of cutting, it was nothing.

I glanced down. The inside of my left arm was covered in tattoos. When I walked in, my arm looked like a chopping block, now it was covered in black-and-blue ink.

I could only see the underlying scars if I looked really close. I guess they would always be part of me. Part of what shaped me. But they no longer identified who I was.

Along these cuts lay words now, words from my own heart:

Always a light will shine
Down upon my life.
Always a hope will spring
And my heart will be full.
Always an angel will sing
As he watches over me.

Where the deepest cut was carved, where I had cut the *A* for my dead brother, blue angel wings were tattooed. Angel wings for my angel brother, Aidan.

As I stood on the sidewalk, beams of sunshine warmed my upturned face.

And I smiled.

acknowledgments

Sometimes I feel like the luckiest girl in the world. To be able to do what I love and have the support of those around me is an incredible, inspiring feeling. I would like to thank Julia, Randi, Mel and Chris for reading these novels and providing me with valuable feedback and gentle critiques. If they didn't love Rowan's stories, I'm not sure this series would have seen the light of day.

I would also like to thank my publisher, BHC Press. I am humbled, moved and so grateful for what they have done for me.

I would like to thank my mom and my Elsie who are the perfect examples of what women and mothers should be.

There would have been no courage to write these novels if it weren't for my three babies, so I would like to thank them for their sweet kisses, tight hugs, and the beautiful way they let me love them.

I would like to thank my husband, Chris. Each time he finishes one of my books, he stumbles toward me, wide-eyed and speechless. After a deep breath, he says, "I don't normally like this genre…but this is a really good book." I love you, honey.

Finally, I would like to thank the readers of these novels. Rowan's story is not an easy one, but I feel it is a story that needs to be told. Rowan may be a fictional character, but her strength is not.

about the author

Tracy Hewitt Meyer is an award-winning author of young adult fiction. Much of her work centers around the challenges teenagers face, and she has tackled the topics of pregnancy, self-harm, and transgender. She holds a B.A. in English and a Master of Social Work. Her other work includes *The Reformation of Marli Meade*, which earned a Gold Medal for Best Regional Fiction from the Independent Publisher Book Awards. Her short story on transgender, "Tender is the Deception," appears in the YA anthology *On the Edge of Tomorrow*. Tracy lives in Virginia with her husband and three children.

Lightning Source UK Ltd.
Milton Keynes UK
UKHW011955061120
372944UK00005B/50/J